"'TELL HIM TO ASK FOR MRS. WILLOUGHBY HAWKINS'"

[Page 25

THE BICYCLERS

AND THREE OTHER FARCES

BY

JOHN KENDRICK BANGS

ILLUSTRATED

NEW YORK
HARPER & BROTHERS PUBLISHERS
1896

CONTENTS

ILLUSTRATIONS

———

Illustrations

THE BICYCLERS

AND THREE OTHER FARCES

THE BICYCLERS

CHARACTERS:

MR. ROBERT YARDSLEY, *an expert.*
MR. JACK BARLOW, *another.*
MR. THADDEUS PERKINS, *a beginner.*
MR. EDWARD BRADLEY, *a scoffer.*
MRS. THADDEUS PERKINS, *a resistant.*
MRS. EDWARD BRADLEY, *an enthusiast.*
JENNIE, *a maid.*

The scene is laid in the drawing-room of Mr. *and* Mrs. Thaddeus Perkins, *at No. — Gramercy Square. It is late October; the action begins at 8.30 o'clock on a moonlight evening. The curtain rising discloses* Mr. *and* Mrs. Perkins *sitting together. At right is large window facing on square. At rear is entrance to drawing - room. Leaning against doorway is a safety bicycle. Perkins is clad in bicycle garb.*

Perkins. Well, Bess, I'm in for it now, and no mistake. Bob and Jack are coming to-night to give me my first lesson in biking.

Mrs. Perkins. I'm very glad of it, Thaddeus. I think it will do you a world of good. You've been working too hard of late, and you need relaxation.

Perkins (doubtfully). I know that—but—from what I can gather, learning to ride a wheel isn't the most restful thing in the world. There's a good deal of lying down about it; but it comes with too great suddenness; that is, so Charlie Cheeseborough says. He learned up at the Academy, and he told me that he spent most of his time making dents in the floor with his head.

Mrs. Perkins. Well, I heard differently. Emma Bradley learned there at the same time he did, and she said he spent most of his time making dents in the floor with other people's heads. Why, really, he drove all the ladies to wearing those odious Psyche knots. The time he ran into Emma, if she hadn't worn her back hair that way she'd have fractured her skull.

Perkins. Ha, ha! They all tell the same story. Barlow said he always wore a beaver hat while Cheeseborough was on the floor, so that if Charlie ran into him and he took a header his brain wouldn't suffer.

Mrs. Perkins. Nevertheless, Mr. Cheeseborough learned more quickly than any one else in the class.

"THOSE ODIOUS PSYCHE KNOTS"

Perkins. So Barlow said—because he wasn't eternally in his own way, as he was in every one else's. (*A ring is heard at the front door.*) Ah! I guess that's Bob and Jack.

Enter Jennie.

Jennie. Mr. Bradley, ma'am.

Perkins. Bradley? Wonder what the deuce he's come for? He'll guy the life out of me. (*Enter* Bradley. *He wears a dinner coat.*) Ah, Brad, old chap, how are you? Glad to see you.

Bradley. Good-evening, Mrs. Perkins. This your eldest?   [*With a nod at* Perkins.

Mrs. Perkins. My eldest?

Bradley. Yes—judged from his togs it was your boy. What! Can it be? You! Thaddeus?

Perkins. That's who I am.

Bradley. When did you go into short trousers?

Perkins (*with a feeble laugh, glancing at his clothes*). Oh, these—ha, ha! I'm taking up the bicycle. Even if it weren't for the exhilaration of riding, it's a luxury to wear these clothes. Old flannel shirt, old coat, old pair of trousers shortened to the knee, and golf stockings. I've had these golf stockings two years, and never had a chance to wear 'em till now.

"'MY ELDEST?'"

Bradley. You've got it bad, haven't you? How many lessons have you had?

Perkins. None yet. Fact is, just got my wheel—that's it over there by the door—pneumatic tires, tool-chest, cyclometer, lamp—all for a hun.

Bradley (with a laugh). How about life-insurance? Do they throw in a policy for that? They ought to.

Perkins. No—but they would if I'd insisted. Competition between makers is so great, they'll give you most anything to induce a bargain. The only thing they really gave me extra is the ki-yi gun.

Mrs. Perkins. The what?

Perkins. Ki-yi gun—it shoots dogs. Dog comes out, catches sight of your leg—

Bradley. Mistakes it for a bone and grabs—eh?

Perkins. Well—I fancy that's about the size of it. You can't very well get off, so you get out your ki-yi gun and shoot ammonia into the beast's face. It doesn't hurt the dog, but it gives him something to think of. I'll show you how the thing works. (*Gets the gun from tool-box*.) This is the deadly weapon, and I'm the rider — see? (*Sits on a chair, with face to back, and works imaginary pedals*.) You're the dog. I'm passing the farm-yard. Bow-wow! out you spring—grab me by the bone—I—ah—I mean the leg. Pouf! I shoot you with ammonia. [*Suits action to the word*.

Bradley (*starting back*). Hi, hold on ! Don't squirt that infernal stuff at me ! My dear boy, get a grip on yourself. I'm not really a ki-yi, and while I don't like bicyclists, their bones are safe from me. I won't bite you.

Mrs. Perkins. Really—I think that's a very ingenious arrangement ; don't you, Mr. Bradley ?

Bradley. I do, indeed. But, as long as we're talking about it, I must say I think what Thaddeus really needs is a motorman-gun, to squirt ammonia, or even beer, into the faces of these cable-car fellows. They're more likely to interfere with him than dogs—don't you think ?

Perkins. It's a first-rate idea, Brad. I'll suggest it to my agent.

Bradley. Your what ?

Perkins (apologetically). Well, I call him my agent, although really I've only bought this one wheel from him. He represents the Czar Manufacturing Company.

Bradley. They make Czars, do they?

THE KI-YI GUN

Perkins (with dignity). They make wheels. The man who owns the company is named Czar. I refer to him as my agent, because from the moment he learned I thought of buying a wheel he came and lived with me. I couldn't get rid of him, and finally in self-defence I bought this wheel. It was the only way I could get rid of him.

Bradley. Aha! That's the milk in the cocoanut, eh? Hadn't force of mind to get rid of the agent. Couldn't say no. Humph! I wondered why you, a man of sense, a man of dignity, a gentleman, should take up with this—

Perkins (angrily). See here, Brad, I like you very much, but I must say—

Mrs. Perkins (foreseeing a quarrel). Thaddeus! 'Sh! Ah, by-the-way, Mr. Bradley, where is Emma this evening? I never knew you to be separated before.

Bradley (sorrowfully). This is the first time, Mrs. Perkins. Fact is, we'd intended calling on you to-night, and I dressed as you see me. Emma was in proper garb too, but when she saw what a beautiful night it was, she told me to go ahead, and she— By Jove! it almost makes me weep!

Perkins. She wasn't taken ill?

Bradley. No—worse. She said: "You go down on the 'L.' I'll bike. It's such a splendid night." Fine piece of business this! To have a bicycle come between man and wife is a pretty hard fate, I think—for the one who doesn't ride.

Mrs. Perkins. Then Emma is coming here?

Bradley. That's the idea, on her wheel — coming down the Boulevard, across Seventy-second Street, through the Park, down Madison, across Twenty-third, down Fourth to Twenty-first, then here.

Perkins. Bully ride that.

Mrs. Perkins. Alone?

Bradley (sadly). I hope so—but these bicyclists have a way of flocking together. For all I know, my beloved Emma may now be coasting down Murray Hill escorted by some bicycle club from Jersey City.

Mrs. Perkins. Oh dear—Mr. Bradley!

Bradley. Oh, it's all right, I assure you, Mrs. Perkins. Perfectly right and proper. It's merely part of the exercise, don't you know. There's a hail-fellow-well-metness about enthusiastic bicyclists, and Emma is intensely enthusiastic. It gives her a chance, you know, and Emma has always wanted a chance. Independence is a thing she's been after ever since she got her freedom, and now, thanks to the wheel, she's got it again, and even I must admit it's harmless. Funny she doesn't get here though (*looking at his watch*); she's had time to come down twice.

[*Bicycle bells are heard ringing without.*

Mrs. Perkins. Maybe that is she now. Go and see, will you, Thaddeus? [*Exit* Perkins.

Perkins (*without*), That you, Mrs. Bradley?

[Mrs. Perkins *and* Bradley *listen intently.*

Two Male Voices. No; it's us, Perk. Got your wheel?

Bradley and *Mrs. Perkins.* Where can she be?

Enter Perkins *with* Barlow *and* Yardsley.

They both greet Mrs. Perkins.

Yardsley. Hullo, Brad! You going to have a lesson too?

Barlow. Dressed for it, aren't you, by Jove! Nothing like a dinner coat for a bicycle ride. Your coat-tails don't catch in the gear.

Bradley (*severely*). I haven't taken it up — fact is, I don't care for fads. Have you seen my wife?

ENTER BARLOW AND YARDSLEY

Yardsley. Yes—saw her the other night at the academy. Rides mighty well, too, Brad. Don't wonder you don't take it up. Contrast, you know—eh, Perk? Fearful thing for a man to have the world see how much smarter his wife is than he is.

Perkins (turning to his wheel). Bradley's a little worried about the non-arrival of Mrs. Bradley. She was coming here on her wheel, and started about the same time he did.

Barlow. Oh, that's all right, Ned. She knows her wheel as well as you know your business. Can't come down quite as fast as the "L," particularly these nights just before election. She may have fallen in with some political parade, and is waiting to get across the street.

Bradley (aside). Well, I like that!

Mrs. Perkins (aside). Why—it's awful!

Yardsley. Or she may possibly have punc-ured her tire—that would delay her fifteen or twenty minutes. Don't worry, my dear boy. I showed her how to fix a punctured tire all right. It's simple enough—you take the rub-ber thing they give you and fasten it in that metal thingumbob, glue it up, poke it in, pull it out, pump her up, and there you are.

Bradley (*scornfully*). You told her that, did you?

Yardsley. I did.

Bradley (*with a mock sigh of relief*). You don't know what a load you've taken off my mind.

Barlow (*looking at his watch*). H'm! Thaddeus, it's nine o'clock. I move we go out and have the lesson. Eh? The moon is just right.

Yardsley. Yes — we can't begin too soon. Wheel all right?

Perkins. Guess so—I'm ready.

Bradley. I'll go out to the corner and see if there's any sign of Mrs. Bradley.   [*Exit.*

Mrs. Perkins (*who has been gazing out of window for some moments*). I do wish Emma would come. I can't understand how women can do these things. Riding down here all alone at night! It is perfectly ridiculous!

Yardsley (*rolling* Perkins's *wheel into middle of room*). Czar wheel, eh?

Perkins (*meekly*). Yes —best going—they tell me.

Barlow. Can't compare with the Alberta. Has a way of going to pieces like the "one-hoss shay"—eh, Bob?

Yardsley. Exactly—when you least expect it, too—though the Alberta isn't much better. You get coasting on either of 'em, and half-way down, bang! the front wheel collapses, hind wheel flies up and hits you in the neck, handle-bar turns just in time to stab you in the chest; and there you are, miles from home, a physical, moral, bicycle wreck. But the Arena wheel is different. In fact, I may say that the only safe wheel is the Arena. That's the one I ride. However, at fifty dollars this one isn't extravagant.

Perkins. I paid a hundred.

Yardsley. A wha—a—at?

Perkins. Hundred.

Barlow. Well you are a—a—good fellow. It's a pretty wheel, anyhow. Eh, Bob?

Yardsley. Simple beauty. Is she pumped up?

Perkins. Beg your pardon?

Yardsley. Pumped up, tires full and tight —ready for action—support an elephant?

Perkins. Guess so—my—I mean, the agent said it was perfect.

Yardsley. Extra nuts?

Perkins. What?

Yardsley. Extra nuts—nuts extra. Suppose you lose a nut, and your pedal comes off; what you going to do—get a tow?

Barlow. Guess Perkins thinks this is like going to sleep.

Perkins. I don't know anything about it. What I'm after is information; only, I give you warning, I will not ride so as to get round shoulders.

Yardsley. Then where's your wrench? Screw up your bar, hoist your handles, elevate your saddle, and you're O.K. What saddle have you?

Perkins (*tapping it*). This.

Barlow. Humph! Not very good—but we'll try it. Come on. It's getting late.

[*They go out.* Perkins *reluctantly. In a moment he returns alone, and, rushing to* Mrs. Perkins, *kisses her affectionately.*

Perkins. Good-bye, dearest.

Mrs. Perkins. Good-bye. Don't hurt yourself, Thaddeus.   [*Exit* Perkins.

Mrs. Perkins (leaving window and looking at clock on mantel). Ten minutes past nine and Emma not here yet. It does seem too bad that she should worry Ed so much just for independence' sake. I am quite sure I should never want to ride a wheel anyhow, and even if I did—

Enter Yardsley *hurriedly, with a piece of flannel in his hand.*

Yardsley. I beg pardon, Mrs. Perkins, but have you a shawl-strap in the house?

Mrs. Perkins (tragically). What is that you have in your hand, Mr. Yardsley?

Yardsley (with a glance at the piece of flannel). That? Oh—ha-ha—that—that's a—ah —a piece of flannel.

Mrs. Perkins (snatching the flannel from Yardsley's *hand).* But Teddy—isn't that a piece of Teddy's—Teddy's shirt?

Yardsley. More than that, Mrs. Perkins. It's the greater part of Teddy's shirt. That's why we want the shawl-strap. When we started him off, you know, he took his coat off. Jack held on to the wheel, and I took Teddy in the fulness of his shirt. One—two

—three! Teddy put on steam—Barlow let go—Teddy went off—I held on—this is what remained. It ruined the shirt, but Teddy is safe. (*Aside.*) Barring about sixty or seventy bruises.

Mrs. Perkins (*with a faint smile*). And the shawl-strap?

Yardsley. I want to fasten it around Teddy's waist, grab hold of the handle, and so hold him up. He's all right, so don't you worry. (*Exit* Mrs. Perkins *in search of shawl-strap.*) Guess I'd better not say anything about the Pond's Extract he told me to bring—doesn't need it, anyhow. Man's got to get used to leaving pieces of his ankle-bone on the curb-stone if he wants to learn to ride a wheel. Only worry her if I asked her for it—won't hurt him to suffer a week.

Enter Bradley.

Bradley. Has she come yet?

Yardsley. No — just gone up-stairs for a shawl-strap.

Bradley. Shawl-strap? Who?

Perkins (*outside*). Hurry up with that Pond's Extract, will you?

"'HAVE YOU A SHAWL-STRAP IN THE HOUSE?'"

Yardsley. All right—coming. Who? Who what?

Bradley. Who has gone up-stairs after shawl-strap—my wife?

Yardsley. No, no, no. Hasn't she got here yet? It's Mrs. Perkins. Perk fell off just now and broke in two. We want to fasten him together.

Barlow (outside). Bring out that pump. His wheel's flabby.

Enter Mrs. Perkins *with shawl-strap.*

Mrs. Perkins. Here it is. What did I hear about Pond's Extract? Didn't somebody call for it?

Yardsley. No—oh no—not a bit of it! What you heard was shawl-strap—sounds like extract—very much like it. In fact—

Bradley. But you did say you wanted—

Yardsley (aside to Bradley). Shut up! Thaddeus banged his ankle, but he'll get over it in a minute. She'd only worry. The best bicyclers in the world are all the time falling off, taking headers, and banging their ankles.

Bradley. Poor Emma!

Enter Barlow.

Barlow. Where the deuce is that Ex—

Yardsley (*grasping him by the arm and pushing him out*). Here it is; this is the ex-strap, just what we wanted. (*Aside to* Bradley.) Go down to the drug-store and get a bottle of Pond's, will you?   [*Exit.*

Mrs. Perkins (*walking to window*). She can't be long in coming now.

Bradley. I guess I'll go out to the corner again. (*Aside.*) Best bicyclers always smashing ankles, falling off, taking headers! If I ever get hold of Emma again, I'll see whether she'll ride that—   [*Rushes out.*

Mrs. Perkins. It seems to have made these men crazy. I never saw such strange behavior in all my life. (*The telephone-bell rings.*) What can that be? (*Goes to 'phone, which stands just outside parlor door.*) Hello! What? Yes, this is 1181—yes. Who are you? What? Emma? Oh dear, I'm so glad! Are you alive? Where are you? What? *Where? The police-station!* (*Turning from telephone.*) Thaddeus, Mr. Barlow, Mr. Yardsley. (*Into telephone.*) Hello! What for? What? Rid-

"'WHERE? THE POLICE STATION!'"

ing without a lamp! Arrested at Forty-second Street! Want to be bailed out? (*Drops
receiver. Rushes into parlor and throws herself
on sofa.*) To think of it—Emma Bradley!
(*Telephone-bell rings violently again;* Mrs.
Perkins *goes to it.*) Hello! Yes. Tell Ed
what? To ask for Mrs. Willoughby Hawkins. Who's she? What, *you!* (*Drops the
receiver; runs to window.*) Thaddeus! Mr.
Yardsley! Mr. Barlow!—all of you come here,
quick.

> [*They rush in.* Perkins *with shawl-strap
> about his waist—limping.* Barlow *has
> large air-pump in his hand.* Mrs. Per-
> kins *grows faint.*

Perkins. Great heavens! What's the matter?

Barlow. Get some water—quick!

> [Yardsley *runs for water.*

Mrs. Perkins. Air! Give me air!

Perkins (*grabbing pump from* Barlow's
hand). Don't stand there like an idiot! Act!
She wants air!

> [*Places pump on floor and begins to pump
> air at her.*

Barlow. Who's the idiot now? Wheel her over to the window. She's not a bicycle.

        [*They do so.* Mrs. Perkins *revives.*

Perkins. What is the matter?

Mrs. Perkins. Mrs. Willoughby Hawkins— arrested — Forty-second Street — no lamp — bailed out. Oh, dear me, dear me! It 'll all be in the papers!

Perkins. What's that got to do with us? Who's Mrs. Willoughby Hawkins?

Mrs. Perkins. Emma! Assumed name.

Barlow. Good Lord! Mrs. Bradley in jail?

Perkins. This is a nice piece of—ow—my ankle, my ankle!

      [*Enter* Bradley *and* Yardsley *at same time,*
          Bradley *with bottle of Pond's Extract,*
          Yardsley *with glass of water.*

Bradley. Where the deuce did you fellows go to? I've been wandering all over the square looking for you.

Perkins. Your wife—

Bradley (*dropping bottle*). What? What about her—hurt?

Mrs. Perkins. Worse!   [*Sobs.*

Bradley. Killed?

Mrs. Perkins. Worse — l-lol-locked up — in jail—no bail—wants to be lamped out.

Bradley. Great heavens! Where?—when? What next? Where's my hat?—what'll the baby say? I must go to her at once.

Yardsley. Hold on, old man. Let me go up. You're too excited. I know the police captain. You stay here, and I'll run up and fix it with him. If you go, he'll find out who Mrs. Hawkins is; you'll get mad, and things will be worse than ever.

Bradley. But—

Barlow. No buts, my dear boy. You just stay where you are. Yardsley's right. It would be an awful grind on you if this ever became known. Bob can fix it up in two minutes with the captain, and Mrs. Bradley can come right back with him. Besides, he can get there in five minutes on his wheel. It will take you twenty on the cars.

Yardsley. Precisely. Meanwhile, Brad, you'd better learn to ride the wheel, so that Mrs. B. won't have to ride alone. This ought to be a lesson to you.

Perkins. Bully idea (*rubbing his ankle*). You

can use my wheel to-night—I—I think I've had enough for the present. (*Aside.*) The pavements aren't soft enough for me; and, O Lord! what a stony curb that was!

Bradley. I never thought I'd get so low.

Yardsley. Well, it seems to me that a man with a wife in jail needn't be too stuck up to ride a bicycle. But—by-by—I'm off. [*Exit.*

Mrs. Perkins. Poor Emma — out for freedom, and lands in jail. What horrid things policemen are, to arrest a woman!

Bradley (*indignantly*). Served her right! If women won't obey the law they ought to be arrested, the same as men. If she wasn't my wife, I'd like to see her sent up for ten years or even twenty years. Women have got no business—

Barlow. Don't get mad, Brad. If you knew the fascination of the wheel you wouldn't blame her a bit.

Bradley (*calming down*). Well—I suppose it has some fascination.

Perkins (*anxious to escape further lessons*). Oh, indeed, it's a most exhilarating sensation: you seem to be flying like a bird over the highways. Try it, Ned. Go on, right away. You don't know how that little ride I had braced me up.

Barlow (with a laugh). There! Hear that! There's a man who's ridden only eight inches in all his life — and he says he felt like a bird!

Perkins (aside). Yes—like a spring chicken split open for broiling. Next time I ride a wheel it 'll be four wheels, with a horse fastened in front. Oh my! oh my! I believe I've broken my back too.   [*Lies down.*

Bradley. You seem to be exhilarated, Thaddeus.

Perkins (bracing up). Oh, I am, I am. Never felt worse—that is, better.

Barlow. Come on, Brad. I'll show you the trick in two jiffies—it 'll relieve your worry about madam, too.

Bradley. Very well—I suppose there's no way out of it. Only let me know as soon as Emma arrives, will you?

Mrs. Perkins. Yes—we will.

[*They go out. As they disappear through the door* Thaddeus *groans aloud.*

Mrs. Perkins. Why—what is the matter, dear? Are you hurt?

Perkins. Oh no—not at all, my love. I was only thinking of Mr. Jarley's indignation to-morrow when he sees the hole I made in his curb-stone with my ankle—oh!—ow!—and as for my back, while I don't think the whole spine is gone, I shouldn't be surprised if it had come through in sections.

Mrs. Perkins. Why, you poor thing—why didn't you say—

Perkins (savagely). Why didn't I say? My heavens, Bess, what did you think I wanted the Pond's Extract for—to drink, or to water the street with? O Lord! (*holding up his arm*). There aren't any ribs sticking out, are there?

Barlow (outside). The other way — there — that's it—you've got it.

Bradley (outside). Why, it *is* easy, isn't it?

Perkins (scornfully). Easy! That fellow'd find comfort in—

Barlow (outside). Now you're off — not too fast.

Mrs. Perkins (walking to window). Why,

Thaddeus, he's going like the wind down the street!

Perkins. Heaven help him when he comes to the river!

Barlow (rushing in). Here we are in trouble again. Brad's gone off on my wheel. Bob's taken his, and your tire's punctured. He doesn't know the first thing about turning or stopping, and I can't run fast enough to catch him. One member of the family is in jail— the other on a runaway wheel!

[Yardsley *appears at door. Assumes attitude of butler announcing guest.*

Yardsley. Missus Willerby 'Awkins!

Enter Mrs. Bradley, *hysterical.*

Mrs. Bradley. Oh, Edward!

[*Throws herself into* Barlow's *arms.*

Barlow (quietly). Excuse me — ah — Mrs. Hawkins — ah — Bradley — but I'm not — I'm not your husband.

Mrs. Bradley (looking up, tragically). Where's Edward?

Mrs. Perkins. Sit down, dear—you must be completely worn out.

Mrs. Bradley (in alarm). Where is he?

Perkins (*rising and standing on one leg*). Fact is, Mrs. Bradley—we don't know. He disappeared ten minutes ago.

"'MISSUS WILLERBY 'AWKINS'"

Yardsley. What do you mean?

Mrs. Bradley. Disappeared?

Barlow. Yes. He went east—at the rate of about a mile a minute.

Mrs. Bradley. My husband—went east? Mile a minute?

Perkins. Yes, on a bike. Yardsley, take me by the shawl-strap, will you, and help me over to that chair; my back hurts so I can't lie down.

Mrs. Bradley. Ned—on a wheel? Why, he can't ride!

Barlow. Oh yes, he can. What I'm afraid of is that he can't stop riding.

Bradley (*outside*). Hi—Barlow—help!

Mrs. Bradley. That's his voice — he called for help.

Yardsley (rushing to window). Hi—Brad—stop! Your wife's here.

Bradley (in distance). Can't stop — don't know how—

Barlow (leaning out of window). By Jove! he's turned the corner all right. If he keeps on around, we can catch him next time he passes.

Mrs. Bradley. Oh, do, do stop him. I'm so afraid he'll be hurt.

Mrs. Perkins (looking out). I can just see him on the other side of the square—and, oh dear me!—*his* lamp is out.

Mrs. Bradley. Oh, Mr. Yardsley—Mr. Barlow—Mr. Perkins—do stop him!

> [*By this time all are gazing out of window, except* Perkins, *who is nursing his ankle.*

Perkins. I guess not. I'm not going to lie down in the road, or sit in the road, or stand in the road to stop him or anybody else. I don't believe I've got a sound bone left; but if I have, I'm going to save it, if Bradley kills himself. If his lamp's out the police will stop him. Why not be satisfied with that?

Bradley (*passing the window*). For Heaven's sake! one of you fellows stop me.

Yardsley. Put on the brake.

Barlow. Fall off. It hasn't got a brake.

Bradley (*despairingly, in distance*). Can't.

Mrs. Perkins. This is frightful.

Perkins (*with a grimace at his ankle*). Yes; but there are other fearful things in this world.

Mrs. Bradley. I shall go crazy if he isn't stopped. He'll kill himself.

Yardsley (*leaving window hurriedly*). I have it. Got a length of clothes-line, Mrs. Perkins?

Barlow. What the dickens—

Mrs. Perkins. Yes.

[*She rushes from the room.*

Mrs. Bradley. What for?

Yardsley. I'll lasso him, next time he comes around.

Perkins (*with a grin*). There'll be two of us! We can start a hospital on the top floor.

Mrs. Perkins (*returning*). Here—here's the line.

" ' POOR, DEAR EDWARD ! ' "

[Yardsley *takes it hurriedly, and, tying it into a noose, hastens out.*

Perkins (rising). If I never walk again, I must see this. [*Limps to window.*

Mrs. Bradley. He's coming, Mr. Yardsley; don't miss him.

Barlow. Steady, Bob; get in the light.

Mrs. Perkins. Suppose it catches his neck?

Perkins. This beats the Wild West Show.

[*A crash.*

All. He's got him.

[*All rush out, except* Perkins.

Perkins. Oh yes; he learned in a minute, he did. Easy! Ha, ha! Gad! it almost makes me forget my pain.

Enter all, asking : " Is he hurt? How do you feel?" *etc.* Yardsley *has rope-end in right hand; noose is tied about* Bradley's *body, his coat and clothing are much the worse for wear.*

Mrs. Bradley. Poor, dear Edward!

Bradley (weakly kissing her). Don't m-mind me. I—I'm all right—only a little exhilarated —and somewhat—er—somewhat breathless. Feel like a bird—on toast. Yardsley, you're a brick. But that pavement—that was a pile of 'em, and the hardest I ever encountered. I always thought asphalt was soft—who said asphalt was soft?

Perkins. Easy to learn, though, eh?

Bradley. Too easy. I'd have gone on—er—forever—er—if it hadn't been for Bob.

Mrs. Bradley. I'll give it up, Ned dear, if you say so.

Mrs. Perkins (affectionately). That's sweet of you, Emma.

Bradley. No, indeed, you won't, for—er—I —I rather like it while it's going on, and when I learn to get off—

Yardsley. Which you will very shortly.

Barlow. You bet! he's a dandy. I taught him.

Bradley. I think I'll adore it.

Perkins. Buy a Czar wheel, Brad. Best in the market; weighs only twenty pounds. I've got one with a ki-yi pump and a pneumatic gun you can have for ten dollars.

Jennie (at the door). Supper is served ma'am.   [*Exit.*

Mrs. Perkins. Let us go out and restore our nerves. Come, Emma.

[*She and* Mrs. Bradley *walk out.*

Yardsley (*aside*). I say, Brad, you owe me five.

Bradley. What for?

Yardsley. Bail.

Barlow. Cheap too.

Yardsley. Very. I think he ought to open a bottle besides.

Perkins. I'll attend to the bottles. We'll have three.

Barlow. Two will be enough.

Perkins. Three—two of fizz for you and Bob and the ladies, and if

" ' KINDLY PRETEND I'M A SHAWL ' "

Bradley will agree, I'll split a quart of Pond's Extract with him.

Bradley. I'll go you. I think I could take care of the whole quart myself.

Perkins. Then we'll make it four bottles.

Mrs. Perkins (appearing at door with her arm about Mrs. Bradley). Aren't you coming?

Perkins (rising with difficulty). As fast as we can, my dear. We've been taking lessons, you know, and can't move as rapidly as the rest of you. We're a trifle—ah—a trifle tired. Yardsley, you tow Bradley into the dining-room ; and, Barlow, kindly pretend I'm a shawl, will you, and carry me in.

Bradley. I'll buy a wheel to-morrow.

Perkins. Don't, Brad. I — I'll give you mine. Fact is, old man, I don't exactly like feeling like a bird.

[*They go out, and as the last,* Perkins *and* Bradley, *disappear stiffly through the portières, the curtain falls.*

A DRAMATIC EVENING

CHARACTERS:

Mr. Thaddeus Perkins, *a victim.*
Mr. Edward Bradley, *a friend in disguise.*
Mr. Robert Yardsley, *an amiable villain.*
Mr. John Barlow, *the amiable villain's assistant.*
Mrs. Thaddeus Perkins, *a martyr.*
Mrs. Edward Bradley, *a woman of executive ability.*
Jennie, *a housemaid.*

The scene is placed in the drawing-room of Mr. *and* Mrs. Thaddeus Perkins, *of New York. The time is a Saturday evening in the early spring, and· the hour is approaching eight. The curtain, rising, discovers* Perkins, *in evening dress, reading a newspaper by the light of a lamp on the table.* Mrs. Perkins *is seated on the other side of the table, buttoning her gloves. Her wrap is on a chair near at hand. The room is gracefully over-furnished.*

Mrs. Perkins. Where are the seats, Thaddeus?

Perkins. Third row; and, by Jove! Bess (*looking at his watch*), we must hurry. It is getting on towards eight now. The curtain rises at 8.15.

Mrs. Perkins. The carriage hasn't come yet. It isn't more than a ten minutes' drive to the theatre.

Perkins. That's true, but there are so many carriage-folk going to see Irving that if we don't start early we'll find ourselves on the end of the line, and the first act will be half over before we can reach our seats.

Mrs. Perkins. I'm so glad we've got good seats—down near the front. I despise opera-glasses, and seats under the galleries are so oppressive.

Perkins. Well, I don't know. For the *Lyons Mail* I think a seat in the front row of the top gallery, where you can cheer virtue and hiss villany without making yourself conspicuous, is the best.

Mrs. Perkins. You don't mean to say that you'd like to sit up with those odious gallery gods?

Perkins. For a melodrama, I do. What's

the use of clapping your gloved hands together at a melodrama? That doesn't express
your feelings. I always want to put two fingers in my mouth and pierce the atmosphere
with a regular gallery-god whistle when I see
the villain laid low by the tow-headed idiot in
the last act—but it wouldn't do in the orches-
tra. You might as well expect the people in
the boxes to eat peanuts as expect an orches-
tra-chair patron to whistle on his fingers.

Mrs. Perkins. I should die of mortification
if you ever should do such a vulgar thing,
Thaddeus.

Perkins. Then you needn't be afraid, my
dear. I'm too fond of you to sacrifice you to
my love for whistling. (*The front-door bell
rings.*) Ah, there is the carriage at last. I'll
go and get my coat.

   [Mrs. Perkins *rises, and is about to don
      her wrap as* Mr. Perkins *goes towards
      the door.*

Enter Mr. *and* Mrs. Bradley. Perkins *stag-
   gers backward in surprise.* Mrs. Perkins
   *lets her wrap fall to the floor, an expression
   of dismay on her face.*

Mrs. Perkins (*aside*). Dear me! I'd forgotten all about it. *This* is the night the club is to meet here!

Bradley. Ah, Perkins, how d' y' do? Glad to see me? Gad! you don't look it.

Perkins. Glad is a word which scarcely expresses my feelings, Bradley. I—I'm simply de-lighted. (*Aside to* Mrs. Perkins, *who has been greeting* Mrs. Bradley.) Here's a kettle of fish. We must get rid of them, or we'll miss the *Lyons Mail.*

Mrs. Bradley. You two are always so formal. The idea of your putting on your dress suit, Thaddeus! It 'll be ruined before we are half through this evening.

Bradley. Certainly, Perkins. Why, man, when you've been moving furniture and taking up carpets and ripping out fireplaces for an hour or two that coat of yours will be a rag—a veritable rag that the ragman himself would be dubious about buying.

Perkins (*aside*). Are these folk crazy? Or am I? (*Aloud.*) Pulling up fireplaces? Moving out furniture? Am I to be dispossessed?

"'GLAD TO SEE ME?'"

Mrs. Bradley. Not by your landlord, but *you* know what amateur dramatics are.

Bradley. I doubt it. He wouldn't have let us have 'em here if he had known.

Perkins. Amateur—amateur dramatics?

Mrs. Perkins. Certainly, Thaddeus. You know we offered our parlor for the performance. The audience are to sit out in the hall.

Perkins. Oh—ah! Why, of course! Certainly! It had slipped my mind; and—ah—what else?

Bradley. Why, we're here to-night to arrange the scene. Don't tell us you didn't know it. Bob Yardsley's coming, and Barlow. Yardsley's a great man for amateur dramatics; he bosses things so pleasantly that you don't know you're being ordered about like a slave. I believe he could persuade a man to hammer nails into his piano-case if he wanted it done, he's so insinuatingly lovely about it all.

Perkins (absently). I'll get a hammer. [*Exit.*

Mrs. Perkins (aside). I must explain to Thaddeus. He'll never forgive me. (*Aloud.*) Thaddeus is so forgetful that I don't believe he can find that hammer, so if you'll excuse me I'll go help him. [*Exit.*

Bradley. Wonder what's up? They don't quarrel, do they?

Mrs. Bradley. I don't believe any one could quarrel with Bessie Perkins—not even a man.

Bradley. Well, they're queer. Acted as if they weren't glad to see us.

Mrs. Bradley. Oh, that's all your imagination. (*Looks about the room.*) That table will have to be taken out, and all these chairs and cabinets; and the rug will never do.

Bradley. Why not? I think the rug will look first-rate.

Mrs. Bradley. A rug like that in a conservatory? [*A ring at the front-door bell is heard.*

Bradley. Ah! maybe that's Yardsley. I hope so. If Perkins and his wife are out of sorts we want to hurry up and get through.

Mrs. Bradley. Oh, we'll be through by twelve o'clock.

Enter Yardsley *and* Barlow.

Yardsley. Ah! here we are at last. The wreckers have arrove. Where's Perkins?

Barlow. Taken to the woods, I fancy. I

say, Bob, don't you think before we begin
we'd better give Perkins ether? He'll suffer
dreadful agony.

Enter Mrs. Perkins, *wiping her eyes.*

Mrs. Perkins. How do you do, Mr. Barlow?
and you, Mr. Yardsley? So glad to see you.
Thaddeus will be down in a minute. He—ah
—he forgot about the—the meeting here to-
night, and he—he put on his dress-coat.

Yardsley. Bad thing to lift a piano in. Better be without any coat. But I say we begin—eh? If you don't mind, Mrs. Perkins.
We've got a great deal to do, and unfortu-
nately hours are limited in length as well as
in number. Ah! that fireplace must be covered up. Wouldn't do to have a fireplace in
a conservatory. Wilt all the flowers in ten
minutes.

Mrs. Perkins (meekly). You needn't have the
fire lit, need you?

Barlow. No—but—a fireplace without fire
in it seems sort of—of bald, don't you think?

Yardsley. Bald? Splendid word applied to
a fireplace. So few fireplaces have hair.

Mrs. Bradley. Oh, it could be covered up

without any trouble, Bessie. Can't we have those dining-room portières to hang in front of it?

Yardsley. Just the thing. Dining-room portières always look well, whether they're in a conservatory or a street scene. (*Enter* Perkins.) Hello, Thaddeus! How d' y'? Got your overalls on?

Perkins (*trying to appear serene*). Yes. I'm ready for anything. Anything I can do?

Bradley. Yes—look pleasant. You look as if you were going to have your picture taken, or a tooth pulled. Haven't you a smile you don't need that you can give us? This isn't a funeral.

Perkins (*assuming a grin*). How'll that do?

Barlow. First-rate. We'll have to make you act next. That's the most villanous grin I ever saw.

Yardsley. I'll write a tragedy to go with it. But I say, Thad, we want those dining-room portières of yours. Get 'em down for us, will you?

Perkins. Dining-room portières! What for?

Mrs. Perkins. They all think the fireplace

would better be hid, Thaddeus, dear. It wouldn't look well in a conservatory.

Perkins. I suppose not. And the dining-room portières are wanted to cover up the fireplace?

Yardsley. Precisely. You have a managerial brain, Thaddeus. *You* can see at once what a dining-room portière is good for. If ever I am cast away on a desert island, with nothing but a dining-room portière for solace, I hope you'll be along to take charge of it. In your hands its possibilities are absolutely unlimited. Get them for us, old man ; and while you are about it, bring a stepladder. (*Exit* Perkins, *dejectedly.*) Now, Barlow, you and Bradley help me with this piano. Pianos may do well enough in gardens or pirates' caves, but for conservatories they're not worth a rap.

Mrs. Bradley. Wait a moment. We must take the bric-à-brac from the top of it before you touch it. If there are two incompatible things in this world, they are men and bric-à-brac.

Mrs. Perkins. You are *so* thoughtful,

though I am sure that Mr. Yardsley would
not break anything willingly.

Barlow. Nothing but the ten command-
ments.

Yardsley. They aren't bric-à-brac; and I
thank you, Mrs. Perkins, for your expression
of confidence. I wouldn't intentionally go
into the house of another man and toss his
Sèvres up in the air, or throw his Royal Wor-
cester down-stairs, except under very great
provocation. (Mrs. Perkins *and* Mrs. Bradley
*have by this time removed the bric-à-brac from
the piano—an upright.*) Now, boys, are you
ready?

Bradley. Where is it to be moved to?

Yardsley. Where would you prefer to have
it, Mrs. Perkins?

Mrs. Perkins. Oh, I have no preference in
the matter. Put it where you please.

Yardsley. Suppose you carry it up into the
attic, Barlow.

Barlow. Certainly. I'll be glad to if you'll
carry the soft pedal. I'm always afraid when
I'm carrying pianos up-stairs of breaking the
soft pedal or dropping a few octaves.

"'I'LL BE GLAD TO IF YOU'LL CARRY THE SOFT PEDAL'"

Yardsley. I guess we'd better put it over in this corner, where the audience won't see it. If you are so careless that you can't move a piano without losing its tone, we'd better not have it moved too far.   Now, then.

> [Barlow, Yardsley, *and* Bradley *endeavor to push the piano over the floor, but it doesn't move.*
> *Enter* Perkins *with two portières wrapped about him, and hugging a small stepladder in his arms.*

Bradley. Hurry up, Perkins.   Don't shirk so.   Can't you see that we're trying to get this piano across the floor?   Where are you at?

Perkins (meekly). I'm trying to make myself at home.   Do you expect me to hang on to these things and move pianos at the same time?

Barlow. Let him alone, Bradley.   He's doing the best he knows.   I always say give a man credit for doing what he can, whether he is intelligent or not.   Of course we don't expect you to hang on to the portières and the stepladder while you are pushing the piano, Thad.   That's too much to expect of any man of your size; some men might do it, but not all.   Drop the portières.

Perkins. Where'll I put 'em?

Yardsley. Put them on the stepladder.

Perkins (*impatiently*). And where shall I put the stepladder—on the piano?

Mrs. Perkins (*coming to the rescue*). I'll take care of these things, Thaddeus, dear.

Bradley. That's right; put everything off on your wife.   What shirks some men are!

Yardsley. Now, then, Perkins, lend us your shoulder, and—one, two, three—push!   Ah! She starts; she moves; she seems to feel the thrill of life along her keel.   We must have gained an inch.   Once more, now.   My, but this is a heavy piano!

Bradley. Must be full of Wagnerian music. Why don't you get a piano of lighter quality, Perkins?   This isn't any kind of an instrument for amateur stage-hands to manage.

Perkins. I'll know better next time.   But is it where you want it now?

Yardsley. Not a bit of it.   We need one more push.   Get her rolling, and keep her rolling until she stands over there in that

corner; and be careful to stop her in time.
I should hate to push a piano through one
of my host's parlor walls just for the want of
a little care. (*They push until the piano stands
against the wall on the other side of the room,
keyboard in.*) There! That's first-rate. You
can put a camp-chair on top of it for the
prompter to sit on; there's nothing like having the prompter up high, because amateur
actors, when they forget their lines, always
look up in the air. Perkins, go sit out in the
hall and imagine yourself an enthusiastic audience—will you?—and tell us if you can see
the piano. If you can see it, we'll have to
put it somewhere else.

Perkins. Do you mean it?

Mrs. Bradley. Of course he doesn't, Mr.
Perkins. It's impossible to see it from the
hall. Now, I think the rug ought to come up.

Mrs. Perkins. Dear me! what for?

Yardsley, Oh, it wouldn't do at all to have
that rug in the conservatory, Mrs. Perkins.
Besides, I should be afraid it would be spoiled.

Perkins. Spoiled? What would spoil it?
Are you going to wear spiked shoes?

Barlow. Spiked shoes? Thaddeus, really you ought to have your mind examined. This scene is supposed to be just off the ballroom, and it is here that Gwendoline comes during the lanciers and encounters Hartley, the villain. Do you suppose that even a villain in an amateur show would go to a ball with spiked shoes on?

Perkins (*wearily*). But I still fail to see what is to spoil the rug. Does the villain set fire to the conservatory in this play, or does he assassinate the virtuous hero here and spill his gore on the floor?

Bradley. What a blood-and-thunder idea of the drama you have! Of course he doesn't. There isn't a death in the whole play, and it's two hours long. One or two people in the audience may die while the play is going on, but people who haven't strong constitutions shouldn't attend amateur shows.

Mrs. Perkins. That's true, I fancy.

Mrs. Bradley. Very. It would be very rude for one of your invited guests to cast a gloom over your evening by dying.

Yardsley. It is seldom done among people

who know what is what. But to explain the point you want explained, Thaddeus: the rug might be spoiled by a leak in the fountain.

Mrs. Perkins. The fountain?

Perkins. You don't mean to say you're going to have a fountain playing here?

Bradley. Certainly. A conservatory without a fountain would be like "Hamlet" with Yorick's skull left out. There's to be a fountain playing here, and a band playing in the next room—all in a green light, too. It 'll be highly effective.

Perkins. But how—how are you going to make the fountain go? Is it to spurt real water?

Yardsley. Of course. Did you ever see a fountain spurt sawdust or lemonade? It's not a soda-water fountain either, but a straight temperance affair, such as you'll find in the homes of all truly good people. Now don't get excited and raise obstacles. The thing is simple enough if you know how to do it. Got one of those English bath-tubs in the house?

Perkins. No. But, of course, if you want a

bath-tub, I'll have a regular porcelain one with running water, hot and cold, put in—two of 'em, if you wish.   Anything to oblige.

Yardsley. No ; stationary bath-tubs are useful, but not exactly adapted to a conservatory.

Barlow. I brought my tub with me. I knew Perkins hadn't one, and so I thought I'd better come provided. It's out in the hall. I'll get it.   [*Exit.*

Mrs. Bradley (*to* Mrs. Perkins). He's just splendid ! never forgets anything.

Mrs. Perkins. I should say not. But, Mr. Yardsley, a bath-tub, even an English one, will not look very well, will it ?

Yardsley. Oh, very. You see, we'll put it in the centre of the room. Just move that table out into the hall, Thaddeus. (*Enter* Barlow *with tub.*) Ah ! now I'll show you. (Perkins *removes table.*) You see, we put the tub here in the middle of the floor, then we surround it with potted plants. That conceals the tub, and there's your fountain.

Perkins. But the water—how do you get that ?

"'YOU SEE, WE PUT THE TUB HERE'"

Bradley. We buy it in bottles, of course, and hire a boy to come in and pour it out every two minutes. How dull you are, Perkins! I'm surprised at you.

Perkins. I'm not over-bright, I must confess, when it comes to building fountains in parlors, with no basis but an English bath-tub to work on.

Yardsley. Did you ever hear of such a thing as a length of hose with a nozzle on one end and a Croton-water pipe at the other, Thaddeus Perkins?

Mrs. Perkins. But where is the Croton-water pipe?

Mrs. Bradley. In the butler's pantry. The hose can be carried through the dining-room, across the hall into this room, and it will be dreadfully effective; and so safe, too, in case the curtain catches fire.

Mrs. Perkins. Oh, Emma! You don't think—

Perkins. Cheerful prospect. But I say, Yardsley, you have arranged for the water supply; how about its exit? How does the water get out of the tub?

Yardsley. It doesn't, unless you want to bore a hole in the floor, and let it flow into the billiard-room below. We've just got to hustle that scene along, so that the climax will be reached before the tub overflows.

Barlow. Perhaps we'd better test the thing now. Maybe my tub isn't large enough for the scene. It would be awkward if the heroine had to seize a dipper and bale the fountain out right in the middle of an impassioned rebuke to Hartley.

Perkins. All right — go ahead. Test it. Test anything. I'll supply the Croton pipes.

Yardsley. None of you fellows happen to have a length of hose with you, do you?

Bradley. I left mine in my other clothes.

Mrs. Bradley. That's just like you men. You grow flippant over very serious matters. For my part, if I am to play Gwendoline, I shall not bale out the fountain even to save poor dear Bessie's floor.

Yardsley. Oh, it 'll be all right. Only, if you see the fountain getting too full, speak faster.

Barlow. We might announce a race between the heroine and the fountain. It would add

"'IT WOULD BE AWKWARD'"

to the interest of the play. This is an athletic age.

Perkins. I suppose it wouldn't do to turn the water off in case of danger.

Barlow. It could be done, but it wouldn't look well. The audience might think the fountain had had an attack of stage fright. Where is the entrance from the ballroom to be.

Yardsley. It ought to be where the fireplace is. That's one reason why I think the portières will look well there.

Mrs. Perkins. But I don't see how that can be. Nobody could come in there. There wouldn't be room behind for any one to stand, would there?

Bradley. I don't know. That fireplace is large, and only two people have to come in that way. The rising curtain discloses Gwendoline just having come in. If Hartley, the villain, and Jack Pendleton, the manly young navy officer, who represents virtue, and dashes in at the right moment to save Gwendoline, could sit close and stand the discomfort of it, they might squeeze in there and await their cues.

Mrs. Perkins. Sit in the fireplace?

Yardsley. Yes. Why not?

Perkins. Don't you interfere, Bess. Yardsley is managing this show, and if he wants to keep the soubrette waiting on the mantelpiece it's his lookout, and not ours.

Yardsley. By-the-way, Thaddeus, Wilkins has backed out, and you are to play the villain.

Perkins. I? Never!

Barlow. Oh, but you must. All you have to do is frown and rant and look real bad.

Perkins. But I can't act.

Bradley. That doesn't make any difference. We don't want a villain that the audience will fall in love with. That would be immoral. The more you make them despise you, the better.

Perkins. Well—I positively decline to sit in the fireplace. I tell you that right now.

Mrs. Bradley. Don't waste time talking about petty details. Let the entrance be there. We can hang the curtain on a frame two feet out from the wall, so that there will be plenty of room behind for Hartley and Pendleton to stand. The frame can be fastened to the

wood-work of the mantel-piece. It may take
a screw or two to hold it, but they'll be high
up, so nobody will notice the holes in the
wood after it comes down. The point that
bothers me is this wall-paper. People don't
put wall-papers on their conservatories.

Perkins (*sarcastically*). I'll have the room
repapered in sheet-glass. Or we might bor-
row a few hot-bed covers and hang them from
the picture moulding, so that the place would
look like a real greenhouse.

Yardsley. Napoleonic idea. Barlow, jot
down among the properties ten hot-bed covers, twenty picture-hooks, and a coil of wire.
You're developing, Perkins.

Mrs. Perkins (*ruefully, aside*). I wish Thaddeus's jokes weren't always taken seriously.
The idea of my drawing-room walls being
hung with hot-bed covers! Why, it's awful.

Yardsley. Well, now that that's settled, we'll
have to dispose of the pictures. Thaddeus,
I wish you'd take down the pictures on the
east wall, so that we can put our mind's eye
on just how we shall treat the background.
The mere hanging of hot-bed covers there

will not do. The audience could see directly through the glass, and the wall-paper would still destroy the illusion.

Perkins. Anything. Perhaps if you got a jack-plane and planed the walls off it would suffice.

Bradley. Don't be sarcastic, my boy. Remember we didn't let you into this. You volunteered.

Perkins. I know it, Bradley. The house is yours.

Barlow. I said you had paresis when you made the offer, Perkins. If you want to go to law about it, I think you could get an injunction against us—or, rather, Mrs. Perkins could—on the ground that you were *non compos* at the time.

Mrs. Perkins. Why, we're most happy to have you, I'm sure.

Perkins. So 'm I. (*Aside.*) Heaven forgive me that!

Yardsley. By-the-way, Thad, there's one thing I meant to have spoken about as soon as I got here. Er—is this *your* house, or do you rent it?

Perkins. I rent it. What has that to do with it?

Bradley. A great deal. You don't think we'd treat *your* house as we would a common landlord's, do you? You wouldn't yourself.

Yardsley. That's the point. If you own the house we want to be careful and consider your feelings. If you *don't*, we don't care what happens.

Perkins. I don't own the house. (*Aside.*) And under the circumstances I'm rather glad I don't.

Yardsley. Well, I'm glad you don't. My weak point is my conscience, and when it comes to destroying a friend's property, I don't exactly like to do it. But if this house belongs to a sordid person, who built it just to put money in his own pocket, I don't care. Barlow, you can nail those portières up. It won't be necessary to build a frame for them. Bradley, carry the chairs and cabinets out.

[Bradley, *assisted by* Perkins, *removes the remaining furniture, placing the bric-à-brac on the floor.*

Barlow. All right.   Where's that stepladder?   Thaddeus, got any nails?

Mrs. Perkins. I—I think we'd rather have a frame, Mr. Yardsley.   *We* can have one made, can't we, Thaddeus?

Perkins. Certainly.   We can have anything made.   (*Aside.*) I suppose I'd build a theatre for 'em if they asked me to, I'm such a confounded—

Yardsley. Oh no.   Of course, if you'd prefer it, we'll send a frame.   I don't think nails would look well in this ceiling, after all.   Temporarily, though, Barlow, you might hang those portières from the picture-moulding.

Barlow. There isn't any.

Yardsley. Well, then, we'll have to imagine how it will look.

Mrs. Bradley. All the bric-à-brac will have to be taken from the room.

Yardsley. True.   Perkins, you know the house better than we do.   Suppose you take the bric-à-brac out and put it where it will be safe.

Perkins. Certainly.

[*Begins to remove bric-à-brac.*

Yardsley. Now let's count up. Here's the fountain.

Barlow. Yes; only we haven't the hose.

Bradley. Well, make a note of it.

Mrs. Perkins. Emma, can't we help Thaddeus?

Mrs. Bradley. Of course. I'll carry out the fender, and you take the andirons.

[*They do so.*

Yardsley. The entrance will be here, and here will be the curtain. How about foot-lights?

Bradley. This bracket will do for a connection. Any plumber can take this bracket off and fasten a rubber pipe to it.

Yardsley. First-rate. Barlow, make a note of one plumber, one length of rubber pipe, and foot-lights.

Bradley. And don't forget to have potted plants and palms, and so forth, galore.

Barlow. No. I'll make a note of that. Will this sofa do for a conservatory?

Yardsley. Jove! Glad you mentioned that. Won't do at all. Thaddeus! (*No answer.*) I hope we haven't driven him to drink.

Bradley. So do I. I'd rather he'd lead us to it.

Yardsley. Thaddeus!

Perkins (from without). Well?

Yardsley. Do you happen to have any conservatory benches in the house?

Mrs. Perkins (appearing in doorway). We have a patent laundry table.

Barlow. Just the thing.

Yardsley (calling). Bring up the patent laundry table, Thaddeus. (*To* Bradley.) What is a patent laundry table?

Bradley. It's what my wife calls the cook's delight. It's an ironing-board on wash-days, a supper table at supper-time, and on the cook's reception days it can be turned into a settee.

Yardsley. It describes well.

Perkins (from a distance). Hi! come down and help me with this thing. I can't carry it up alone.

Yardsley. All right, Perk. Bradley, you and Barlow help Thaddeus. I'll move these other chairs and tables out. It's getting late, and we'll have to hustle.

[*Exit* Barlow. Bradley *meanwhile has been removing pictures from the walls, and, as* Yardsley *speaks, is standing on the stepladder reaching up for a painting.*

Bradley. What do you take me for—twins?

Yardsley. Don't get mad, now, Bradley. If there's anything that can add to the terror of amateur theatricals it's temper.

Mrs. Bradley (from without). Edward, come here right away. I want you to move the hat-stand, and see how many people can be seated in this hall.

Bradley. Oh yes, certainly, my dear — of course. Right away. My name is Legion— or Dennis.

Yardsley. That's the spirit. (*A crash is heard without.*) Great Scott! What's that?

Mrs. Perkins (without). Oh, Thaddeus!

Bradley. They've dropped the cook's delight.

[*He comes down from the stepladder. He and* Yardsley *go out. The pictures are piled up on the floor, the furniture is topsy-turvy, and the portières lie in a heap on the hearth.*

Enter Mrs. Perkins.

Mrs. Perkins. Dear, dear, dear! What a mess! And poor Thaddeus! I'm glad he wasn't hurt; but I—I'm afraid I heard him say words I never heard him say before when Mr. Barlow let the table slip. Wish I hadn't said anything about the table.

Enter Mrs. Bradley.

Mrs. Bradley. These men will drive me crazy. They are making more fuss carrying that laundry table up-stairs than if it were a house; and the worst of it is our husbands are losing their tempers.

Mrs. Perkins. Well, I don't wonder. It must be awfully trying to have a laundry table fall on you.

Mrs. Bradley. Oh, Thaddeus is angelic, but Edward is absolutely inexcusable. He swore a minute ago, and it sounded particularly profane because he had a screw and a picture-hook in his mouth.

Yardsley (outside). It's almost as heavy as the piano. I don't see why, either.

[*The four men appear at the door, staggering under the weight of the laundry table.*

Perkins (*as they set it down*). Whew! That's what I call work. What makes this thing so heavy?

Mrs. Bradley (*as she opens a drawer and takes out a half-dozen patent flat-irons and a handle*). This has something to do with it. Why didn't you take out the drawer first?

Yardsley. It wasn't my fault. They'd started with it before I took hold. *I* didn't know it had a drawer, though I did wonder what it was that rattled around inside of it.

Bradley. It wasn't for me to suggest taking the drawer out. Thaddeus ought to have thought of that.

Perkins (*angrily*). Well, of all—

Mrs. Perkins. Never mind. It's here, and it's all right.

Yardsley. That's so. We musn't quarrel. If we get started, we'll never stop. Now, Perkins, roll up that rug, and we'll get things placed, and then we'll be through.

Barlow. Come on; I'll help. Bradley, get those pictures off the rug. Don't be so careless of Mrs. Perkins's property.

Bradley. Careless? See here now, Barlow—

Mrs. Bradley. Now, Edward — no temper. Take the pictures out.

Bradley. And where shall I take the pictures out to ?

Yardsley. Put 'em on the dining-room table.

Perkins (*aside*). Throw 'em out the window, for all I care.

Bradley. Eh ?

Perkins. Nothing. I—er—I only said to put 'em—er—to put 'em wherever you pleased.

Bradley. But *I* can't say where they're to go, Thaddeus.   This isn't my house.

Perkins (*aside*). No—worse luck—it's mine.

Mrs. Perkins. Oh—put them in the dining-room ; they'll be safe there.

Bradley. I will.

> [*He begins carrying the pictures out.* Perkins, Barlow, *and* Yardsley *roll up the rug.*

Yardsley. There ! You fellows might as well carry that out too; and then we'll be ready for the scene.

Barlow. Come along, Thaddeus.   You're earning your pay to-night.

"'THIS HAS SOMETHING TO DO WITH IT'"

Perkins (*desperately*). May I take my coat off? I'm boiling.

Mrs. Bradley. Certainly. I wonder you didn't think of it before.

Perkins. Think? I never think.

Yardsley. Well, go ahead in your thoughtless way and get the rug out. You are delaying us.

Perkins. All right. Come on. Barlow, are you ready?

Barlow. I am.   [*They drag the rug out.*

Yardsley. At last. (*Replaces the tub.*) There's the fountain. Now where shall we put the cook's delight?

Mrs. Perkins. Over here, I should say.

Mrs. Bradley. *I* think it would be better here.

Bradley (*who has returned*). Put it half-way between 'em, Yardsley. I say give in always to the ladies; and when they don't agree, compromise. It's a mighty poor woman that isn't half right occasionally.

Mrs. Bradley. Edward!

Yardsley (*adopting the suggestion*). There! How's that?

Perkins (returning). Perfect. I never saw such an original conservatory in my life.

Mrs. Perkins. I suppose it's all right. What do you think, Emma?

Mrs. Bradley. Why, it's simply fine. Of course it requires a little imagination to see it as it will be on the night of the perform-ance; but in general I don't see how it could be better.

Barlow. No—nor I. It's great as it is, but when we get the hot-bed covers hung, and the fountain playing, and plants arranged gracefully all around, it will be ideal. I say we ought to give Yardsley a vote of thanks.

Perkins. That's so. We're very much in-debted to Yardsley.

Yardsley. Never mind that. I enjoy the work very much.

Perkins. So glad. (*Aside.*) I wonder when *we* get a vote of thanks?

Bradley (looking at his watch). By Jove, Emma, it's after eleven!

Mrs. Bradley. After eleven? Dear me! I had no idea it was as late as that. How time flies when you are enjoying yourself! Really, Edward, you ought not to have overlooked the time. You know—

Bradley. I supposed you knew we couldn't pull a house down in five minutes.

Perkins. What's become of the clock?

Mrs. Perkins. I don't know. Who took the clock out?

Barlow. I did. It's under the dining-room table.

Mrs. Bradley. Well, we mustn't keep Bessie up another moment. Good-night, my dear. We have had a delightful time.

Mrs. Perkins. Good-night. I am sure we have enjoyed it.

Perkins (*aside*). Oh yes, indeed; *we* haven't had so much fun since the children had the mumps.

Yardsley. Well, so-long, Perkins. Thanks for your help.

Perkins. By-by.

Barlow. Good-night.

Yardsley. Don't bother about fixing up to-night, Perkins. I'll be around to-mor-

row evening and help put things in order
again.

> [*They all go out. The good-nights are
> repeated, and finally the front door is
> closed.*

Re-enter Perkins, *who falls dejectedly on the
settee, followed by* Mrs. Perkins, *who gives a
rueful glance at the room.*

Perkins. I'm glad Yardsley's coming to fix
us up again. I *never* could do it.

Mrs. Perkins. Then I must. I can't ask
Jennie to do it, she'd discharge us at once,
and I can't have my drawing-room left this
way over Sunday.

Perkins (wearily). Oh, well, shall we do it
now ?

Mrs. Perkins. No, you poor dear man ; we'll
stay home from church to-morrow morning
and do it. It won't be any harder work than
reading the Sunday newspapers. What have
you there ?

*Perkins (looking at two tickets he has abstract-
ed from his vest-pocket).* Tickets for Irving—
this evening—*Lyons Mail*—third row from
the stage. I was just thinking—

Mrs. Perkins. Don't tell me what you were thinking, my dear. It can't be expressible in polite language.

Perkins. You are wrong there, my dear. I wasn't thinking cuss-words at all. I was only

"'HE'S BEEN THERE THREE HOURS NOW'"

reflecting that we didn't miss much anyhow, under the circumstances.

Mrs. Perkins. Miss much? Why, Thaddeus, what *do* you mean?

Perkins. Nothing — only that for action continuous and situations overpowering the

Lyons Mail isn't a marker to an evening of preparation for Amateur Dramatics.

              Enter Jennie.

Jennie. Excuse me, mim, but the coachman says shall he wait any longer? He's been there three hours now.

[CURTAIN]

THE FATAL MESSAGE

CHARACTERS:

MR. THADDEUS PERKINS, *in charge of the curtain.*
MRS. THADDEUS PERKINS, *cast for Lady Ellen.*
MISS ANDREWS, *cast for the maid.*
MR. EDWARD BRADLEY, *an under-study.*
MRS. EDWARD BRADLEY, *cast for Lady Amaranth.*
MR. ROBERT YARDSLEY, *stage-manager.*
MR. JACK BARLOW, *cast for Fenderson Featherhead.*
MR. CHESTER HENDERSON, *an absentee.*
JENNIE, *a professional waitress.*

The scene is laid in the library of the Perkins *mansion, on the afternoon of the day upon which an amateur dramatic performance is to be held therein. The* Perkins *house has been given over to the dramatic association having the matter in charge. At right of library a scenic doorway is hung. At left a drop-curtain is arranged, behind which is the middle hall of the* Perkins *dwelling, where the expected audience are to sit. The unoccupied wall spaces are hung with paper-muslin.*

The apartment is fitted up generally to resemble an English drawing-room ; table and chair at centre.   At rear stands a painted-canvas conservatory entrance, on left of which is a long oaken chest.   The curtain rising discovers Mrs. Perkins *giving a few finishing touches to the scene, with* Mr. Perkins *gazing curiously about the room.*

Perkins. Well, they've transformed this library into a scene of bewitching beauty—haven't they?   These paper-muslin walls are a dream of loveliness.   I suppose, as the possessor of all this, I ought to be supremely happy—only I wish that canvas conservatory door hadn't been tacked over my reference-books. I want to look up some points about—

Mrs. Perkins. Oh, never mind your books, Thaddeus ; it's only for one night.   Can't you take a minute's rest ?

Perkins. One night ?   I like that.   It's been there two already, and it's in for to-night, and all day to-morrow, I suppose.   It'll take all day to-morrow to clean up, I'll wager a hat.

I'm beginning to rue the hour I ever allowed the house of Perkins to be lured into the drama.

Mrs. Perkins. You're better off than I am. I've got to take part, and I don't half know my lines.

Perkins. I? I better off? I'd like to know if I haven't got to sit out in front and watch you people fulfil your diabolical mission in your doubly diabolical way, and grin at the fearful jokes in the dialogue I've been listening to for weeks, and make the audience feel that they are welcome when they're not. What's been done with my desk?

Mrs. Perkins. It's down in the laundry. You're about as—

Perkins. Oh, is it? Laundry is a nice place for a desk. Plenty of starch handy to stiffen up a writer's nerve, and scrubbing-boards galore to polish up his wits. And I suppose my papers are up in the attic?

Mrs. Perkins. No; they're stowed away safely in the nursery. Now please don't complain!

Perkins. Me? Complain? I never complain.

I didn't say a word when Yardsley had my Cruikshanks torn from their shelves and chucked into a clothes-basket and carried into the butler's pantry, did I? Did I say as much as one little word? I wanted to say one little word, I admit, but I didn't. Did I? If I did, I withdraw it. I'm fond of this sort of thing. The greatest joy in life is to be found in arranging and rearranging a library, and I seem to be in for joy enough to kill. What time are the—these amateur Thespians coming?

Mrs. Perkins (looking at her watch). They're due now; it's half-past four. (*Sits down and opens play-book. Rehearses.*) No, not for all the world would I do this thing, Lord Muddleton. There is no need to ask it of me. I am firm. I shall—

Perkins. Oh, let up, my dear! I've been getting that for breakfast, dinner, and tea for two weeks now, and I'm awfully tired of it. When I asked for a second cup of coffee at breakfast Sunday, you retorted, "No, not for all the world would I do this thing, Lord Muddleton!" When I asked you where my dress ties were, you informed me that it was "what baseness," or words to that effect; and so on, until I hardly know where I am at. (*Catches sight of the chest.*) Hello! How did that happen to escape the general devastation? What are you going to do with that oak chest?

Mrs. Perkins. It is for the real earl to hide in just before he confronts Muddleton with the evidence of his crime.

Perkins. But — that holds all my loose prints, Bess. By Jove! I can't have that, you know. You amateur counterfeiters have got to understand just one thing. I'll submit to the laundering of my manuscripts, the butler's-pantrying of my Cruikshanks, but I'll be hanged if I'll allow even a real earl, much less a base imitation of one, to wallow in my engravings.

Mrs. Perkins. You needn't worry about your old engravings. They're perfectly safe. I've put them in the Saratoga trunk in the attic. (*Rehearsing.*) And if you ask it of me once again, I shall have to summon my servants to have you shown the door. Henry Cobb is the friend of my girlhood, and—

Perkins. Henry Cobb be—

Mrs. Perkins. Thaddeus!

Perkins. I don't care, Bess, if Henry Cobb was the only friend you ever had. I object to having my prints dumped into a Saratoga trunk in order that he may confront Muddleton and regain the lost estates of Puddingford by hiding in my chest. A gay earl Yardsley makes, anyhow; and as for Barlow, he looks like an ass in that yellow-chrysanthemum wig. No man with yellow hair like that could track such a villain as Henderson makes Muddleton out to be. Fact is, Henderson is the only decent part of the show.

Mrs. Perkins (rehearsing). What if he is weak? Then shall I still more strongly show myself his friend. Poor? Does not—

Perkins. Oh, I suppose it does— (*Bell rings.*) There comes this apology for a real earl, I fancy. I'll let him in myself. I suppose Jennie has got as much as she can do sweeping my manuscripts out of the laundry, and keeping my verses from scorching the wash.   [*Exit.*

Mrs. Perkins. It's too bad of Thaddeus to go on like this. As if I hadn't enough to worry me without a cross husband to manage. Heigho!

Enter Perkins *with* Yardsley. Yardsley *holds bicycle cap in hand.*

Yardsley. By Jove! I'm tired. Everything's been going wrong to-day. Overslept myself, to begin with, and somebody stole my hat at the club, and left me this bicycle cap in its place. How are you getting along, Mrs. Perkins? You weren't letter perfect yesterday, you know.

Mrs. Perkins. I'm getting it all right, I think. I've been rehearsing all day.

Perkins. You bet your life on that, Henry Cobb, real Earl of Puddingford. If you aren't restored to your estates and title this night, it won't be for any lack of suffering on my part. Give me your biking cap, unless you want to use it in the play. I'll hang it up. [*Exit.*

Yardsley. Thanks. (*Looks about the room.*) Everything here seems to be right.

Perkins *returns.*

Mrs. Perkins. (*rehearsing*). And henceforth, my lord, let us understand one another.

Perkins. Certainly, my dear. I'll go and

have myself translated. Would you prefer me in French, German, or English?

Yardsley. I hope it goes all right to-night. But, I must say, I don't like the prospect. This beastly behavior of Henderson's has knocked me out.

Perkins. What's the matter with Henderson?

Mrs. Perkins. He hasn't withdrawn, has he?

Yardsley. That's just what he has done. He sent me word this morning.

Mrs. Perkins. But what excuse does he offer? At the last moment, too!

Yardsley. None at all—absolutely. There was some airy persiflage in his note about having to go to Boston at six o'clock. Grandmother's sick or something. He writes so badly I couldn't make out whether she was rich or sick. I fancy it's a little of both. Possibly if she wasn't rich he wouldn't care so much when she fell ill. That's the trouble with these New-Englanders, anyhow—they've always got grandmothers to fall down at crucial moments. Next time I go into this sort of thing it'll be with a crowd without known ancestors.

Perkins. 'Tisn't Chet's fault, though. You don't suspect him of having poisoned his grandmother just to get out of playing, do you ?"

Mrs. Perkins. Oh, Thaddeus, do be serious !

Perkins. I was never more so, my dear. Poisoning one's grandmother is no light crime.

Yardsley, Well, I've a notion that the whole thing is faked up. Henderson has an idea that he's a little tin Booth, and just because I called him down the other night at our first rehearsal he's mad. That's the milk in the cocoanut, I think. He's one of those fellows you can't tell anything to, and when I kicked because he wore a white tie with a dinner coat, he got mad and said he was going to dress the part his own way or not at all.

Perkins. I think he was right.

Yardsley. Oh yes, of course I'm never right. What am I stage-manager for ?

Perkins. Oh, as for that, of course, you are the one in authority, but you were wrong about the white tie and the dinner coat. He was a bogus earl, an adventurer, wasn't he?

Yardsley. Yes, he was, but—

Perkins. Well, no real earl would wear a white tie with a dinner coat unless he were visiting in America. I grant you that if he were going to a reception in New York he might wear a pair of golf trousers with a dinner coat, but in this instance his dress simply showed his bogusity, as it were. He merely dressed the part.

Yardsley. He doesn't want to make it too plain, however, so I was right after all. His villany is to come as a painful surprise.

Mrs. Perkins. But what are we to do? Have you got anybody else to take his part?

Yardsley. Yes. I telegraphed right off to Bradley, explained as far as I could in a telegram without using all the balance in the treasury, and he answered all right. Said he'd bone at the part all day, and would be here at five letter perfect.

Mrs. Perkins (with a sigh of relief). Good. He's very quick at learning a thing. I imagine it will be all right. I've known him to

learn a harder part than that in five hours.
It 'll be pleasanter for Emma, too. She didn't
like those scenes she had as Lady Amaranth
the adventuress with Henderson. He kept
her off the middle of the stage all the time;
but with her husband it will be different.

Perkins. I'll bet on that! No good-natured
husband of a new women ever gets within a
mile of the centre of the stage while she's on
it. She'll have stage room to burn in her
scenes with Brad.

Mrs. Perkins. I think it was awfully mean
of Mr. Henderson, though.

Yardsley. Disgusting.

Perkins. It was inconsiderate. So hard on
his grandmother, too, to be compelled to
knock under just to get him out of a disagree-
ble situation. She ought to disinherit him.

Yardsley. Oh, it's easy enough to be sarcastic.

Perkins. That's so, Bob; that's why I never
am. It's commonplace. (*Bell rings.*) Ah,
there's the rest of the troupe, I guess. [*Exit.*

Yardsley (*looking at his watch*). It's about
time. They're twenty minutes late.

Mrs. Perkins. (reheasing). So once for all, Lord Muddleton—*(derisively)*—ha, ha! Lord Muddleton! that *is* amusing. You — Lord Muddleton! Ha, ha! Once for all, Lord Muddleton, I acquaint you with my determination. I shall not tell Henry Cobb what I have discovered, since I have promised, but none the less he shall know. Walls have ears—even that oaken chest by yinder wonder—

Yardsley (irritated). Excuse me, Mrs. Perkins; but really you must get that phrase right. You've called it yinder wonder at every rehearsal we've had so far. I know it's difficult to get right. Yonder window is one of those beastly combinations that playwrights employ to make the Thespian's pathway to fame a rocky one; but you must get over it, and say it right. Practise it for an hour, if need be—yonder window, yonder winder—I mean, yonder window—until it comes easy.

Mrs. Perkins (meekly). I have, and it doesn't seem to do any good. I've tried and tried to get it right, but yonder window is all I can say.

Yardsley. But yinder window is—I should say, yonder window is correct.

Mrs. Perkins. Well, I'm just going to change it, that's all. It shall be yonder casement.

Yardsley. Good idea. Only don't say yonder basement by mistake.

Enter Perkins, *followed by* Barlow.

Perkins. Here's Mr. Featherhead. He's rehearsing too. As I opened the door he said, "Give me good-morrow."

Barlow (smiling). Yes; and Thaddeus replied, "Good-yesterday, me friend," in tones which reminded me of Irving with bronchitis. What's this I hear about Henderson's grandmother?

Yardsley. Thrown up the part.

Barlow. His grandmother?

Yardsley. No — idiot — Henderson. He's thrown up his grandmother—oh, hang it!— you know what I mean.

Mrs. Perkins. I hope you're not going to net gervous, Mr. Yardsley. If you break down, what on earth will become of the rest of us?

Yardsley. I hope not—but I am. I'm as

nervous as a cat living its ninth life. Here
we are three or four hours before the performance, and no one knows whether we'll be
able to go through it or not. My reputation
as a manager is at stake. Barlow, how are
you getting along on those lines in the rev-
elation scene?

Barlow. Had 'em down fine on the cable-
car as I came up. Ha-ha! People thought I
was crazy, I guess. I was so full of it I kept
repeating it softly to myself all the way up;
but when we got to that Fourteenth Street
curve the car gave a fearful lurch and fairly
shook the words "villanous viper" out of
me; and as I was standing when we began
the turn, and was left confronting a testy old
gentleman upon whose feet I had trodden
twice, at the finish, I nearly got into trouble.

Perkins (with a laugh). Made a scene, eh?

Barlow (joining in the laugh). Who
wouldn't? Each time I stepped on his foot
he glared—regular Macbeth stare—like this:
"Is this a jagger which I see before me?"
(*Suits action to word.*) But I never let on I
saw, but continued to rehearse. When the

lurch came, however, and I toppled over on top of him, grabbed his shoulders in my hands to keep from sprawling in his lap, and hissed "villanous viper" in his face, he was inclined to resent it forcibly.

Yardsley. I don't blame him. Seems to me a man of your intelligence ought to know better than to rehearse on a cable-car, anyhow, to say nothing of stepping on a man's corns.

Barlow. Of course I apologized ; but he was a persistent old codger, and demanded an explanation of my epithet.

Perkins. It's a wonder he didn't have you put off. A man doesn't like to be insulted even if he does ride on the cable.

Barlow. Oh, I appeased him. I told him I was rehearsing. That I was an amateur actor.

Mrs. Perkins. And of course he was satisfied.

Barlow. Yes ; at least I judge so. He said that my confession was humiliation enough, without his announcing to the public what he thought I was ; and he added, to the man next him, that he thought the public was exposed to enough danger on the cable cars without having lunatics thrust upon them at every turning.

Perkins. He must have been a bright old man.

Mrs. Perkins. Or a very crabbed old person.

Barlow. Oh, well, it was an experience, but it rather upset me, and for the life of me I haven't been able to remember the opening lines of the scene since.

Perkins. Well, if the audience drive you off the stage, you can sue the cable company. They ought to be careful how they lurch a man's brains out.

Yardsley. That's right — joke ahead. It's fun for you. All you've got to do is to sit out in front and pull the curtain up and down when we ring a bell. You're a great one to talk about brains, you are. It's a wonder to me you don't swoon under your responsibility.

Mrs. Perkins (*rehearsing*). So once for all, as he says, so say I—

Perkins. Ah! Indeed! You take his part, do you?

Mrs. Perkins (*rehearsing*). You must leave this house at once and forever. I once thought

I loved you, but now all is changed, and I take this opportunity to thank my deliverer, Fenderson Featherhead—

Perkins. Oh — ah — rehearsing. I see. I thought you'd gone over to the enemy, my dear. Featherhead, step up and accept the lady's thanks. Cobb, join me in the dining-room, and we'll drown our differences in tasting the punch, which, between you and me, is likely to be the best part of to-night's function, for I made it myself—though, if Tom Harkaway is in the audience, and Bess follows out her plan of having the flowing bowl within reach all the evening, I'm afraid it'll need an under-study along about nine o'clock. He's a dry fellow, that Harkaway.

[*Exit* Perkins, *dragging* Yardsley *by the arm.*

Barlow (*calling after them*). Don't you touch it, Bob. It's potent stuff. One glass may postpone the performance.

Yardsley (*from behind the scenes*). Never fear for me, my boy. I've got a head, I have.

Barlow. Well, don't get another. (*Turning to* Mrs. Perkins.) Suppose we rehearse that scene where I acquaint you with Cobb's real position in life?

Mrs. Perkins. Very well. I'm ready. I'm to sit here, am I not?   [*Seats herself by table.*

Barlow. And I come in here. (*Begins.*) Ah, Lady Ellen, I am glad to find you alone, for I have that to say—

Mrs. Perkins. Won't you be seated, Mr. Featherhead? It was such a delightful surprise to see you at the Duchess of Barncastle's last evening. I had supposed you still in Ireland.

Barlow (aside). Good. She little thinks that I have just returned from Australia, where I have at last discovered the identity of the real Earl of Puddingford, as well as that of this bogus Muddleton, who, by his nefarious crime, has deprived Henry Cobb of his patrimony, of his title, aye, even of his name. She little wots that this—this adventurer who has so strongly interested her by his nepotic—

Mrs. Perkins (interrupting). Hypnotic, Mr. Barlow.

Barlow. What did I say?

Mrs. Perkins. Nepotic.

Barlow. How stupid of me! I'll begin again.

Mrs. Perkins (*desperately*). Oh, pray don't.
Go on from where you left off. That's a fear-
fully long aside, anyhow, and I go nearly crazy
every time you say it. I don't know what to
do with myself. It's easy enough for Mr.
Yardsley to say occupy yourself somehow, but
what I want to know is, how? I can't look inquiringly at you all that time, waiting for you
to say " Ireland! Oh, yes—yes—just over from
Dublin." I can't lean against the mantel-piece
and gaze into the fire, because the mantel-
piece is only canvas, and would fall down if I
did.

Barlow. It's a long aside, Mrs. Perkins, but
it's awfully important, and I don't see how we
can cut it down. It's really the turning-point
of the play, in which I reveal the true state of
affairs to the audience.

Mrs. Perkins (*with a sigh*). I suppose that's
true. I'll have to stand it. But can't I be
doing some sewing?

Barlow. Certainly not. You are the daugh-
ter of a peer. They never sew. You might
be playing a piano, but there's hardly room on

the stage for that, and, besides, it would interfere with my aside, which needs a hush to be
made impressive.   Where did I leave off?

Mrs. Perkins. Hypnotic power.

Barlow. Oh yes. (*Resumes rehearsing.*) She
little wots that this—this adventurer who has
so strangely interested her with his hypnotic
power is the man who twenty years ago forged
her father's name to the title-deeds of Burn-
ington, drove him to his ruin, and subsequent-
ly, through a likeness so like as to bewilder
and confuse even a mother's eyes, has forced
the rightful Earl of Puddingford out into a
cruel world, to live and starve as Henry Cobb.

[*Bell.*

Mrs. Perkins. Ah, I fancy the Bradleys are
here at last.   I do hope Edward knows his part.

Enter Yardsley.

Yardsley. They've come, and we can begin
at last.

Enter Perkins, Miss Andrews, *and* Mr. *and*
Mrs. Bradley.

Mrs. Perkins. Take off your things, Emma.
Let me take your cloak, Dorothy.   Does Edward feel equal—

Mrs. Bradley. He says so.   Knows it word for word, he says, though I've been so busy with my own—   [*They go out talking.*

Yardsley. Well, Brad, how goes it?   Know your part?

Bradley. Like a book.   Bully part, too.

Barlow. Glad you like it.

Bradley. Can't help liking it ; it's immense! Particularly where I acquaint the heroine with the villany that—

Barlow. You?   Why—

Enter Mrs. Bradley, Miss Andrews, *and* Mrs. Perkins.

Mrs. Perkins (*to* Bradley). So glad you're going to play with us.

Bradley. So am I.   It's a great pleasure. Felt rather out in the cold until—

Barlow. But, I say, Brad, you don't—

Yardsley. Howdy do, Mrs. Bradley?   Good-afternoon, Miss Andrews.   We all seem to be here now, so let's begin.   We're a half-hour late already.

Barlow. I'm ready, but I want to—

Yardsley. Never mind what you want, Jack. We haven't time for any more talking.   It 'll take us an hour and a half, and we've got to hustle. All off stage now except Mrs. Perkins. (*All go out;* Yardsley *rings bell.*) Hi, Perkins, that's your cue!

Perkins. What for?

Yardsley. Oh, hang it!—raise the curtain, will you?

Perkins. With pleasure. As I understand this thing, one bell signifies raise curtain when curtain's down; drop curtain when curtain is up.

Yardsley. Exactly. You know your part, anyhow. If you remember not to monkey with the curtain except when the bell rings, and then change its condition, no matter what it may be, you can't go wrong. Now begin. (*Bell.* Perkins *raises curtain.*) Now, of course, I'm not supposed to be on the stage, but I'll stay here and prompt you. Enter Lady Ellen. Come along, Mrs. Perkins. Please begin.

Mrs. Perkins. I thought we'd decided that I was to be sitting here when the curtain went up?

Yardsley. So we did. I'd forgotten that.

We'll begin all over again. Perkins, drop that curtain. Perkins!

Perkins. What?

Yardsley. Drop the curtain.

Perkins. Where's the bell? I didn't hear any bell ring.

Yardsley. Oh, never mind the bell! Let her down.

Perkins. I beg your pardon, but I positively refuse. I believe in doing things right. I'm not going to monkey. Ring that bell, and down she comes; otherwise—

Yardsley. Tut! You are very tiresome this afternoon, Thaddeus. Mrs. Perkins, we'll go ahead without dropping the curtain. Now take your place.

[Mrs. Perkins *seats herself by table, picks up a book, and begins to read.*

Mrs. Perkins (after an interval, throwing book down with a sigh). Heigho! I cannot seem to concentrate my mind upon anything to-night. I wonder why it is that once a woman gives her heart into another's keeping— [*Bell rings.* Perkins *lets curtain drop.*

Vardsley. What the deuce did you drop that curtain for, Thaddeus?

Perkins. The bell rang, didn't it?

Vardsley. Yes, you idiot, but that's supposed to be the front-door bell.   Lady Amaranth is about to arrive—

Perkins. Well, how was I to know?   Your instructions to me were positive.   Don't monkey with curtain till bell rings.   When bell rings, if down, pull her up; if up, pull her down.   I'm not a connoisseur on bells—

Vardsley. You might pay some attention to the play.

Perkins. Now look here, Bob.   I don't want to quarrel with you, but it seems to me that I've got enough to do without paying attention to your part of the show.   What am I? First place, host; second place, head usher; third place, curtain - manager; fourth place, fire department; fifth place, Bess says if children holler, go up and see what's the matter —other words, nurse—and on top of this you say keep an eye on the play.   You must think I've as many eyes as a President's message.

Mrs. Perkins. Oh dear, Teddy! do behave. It's simple enough—

Perkins. Simple enough? Well, I like that. How am I to tell one bell from another if—

Yardsley (dryly). I suppose if the clock strikes ten you'll seesaw the curtain up and down ten times, once for each stroke—eh?

Bradley (poking his head in at the door). What's the matter in here? Emma's been waiting for her cue like a hundred-yards runner before the pistol.

Perkins. Oh, it's the usual trouble with Yardsley. He wants me to chaperon the universe.

Yardsley. It's the usual row with you. You never want to do anything straight. You seem to think that curtain's an elevator, and you're the boy—yanking it up and down at your pleasure, and—

Mrs. Perkins. Oh, please don't quarrel! Can't you see, Ted, it's growing late? We'll never have the play rehearsed, and it's barely three hours now before the audience will arrive.

Perkins. Very well — I'll give in — only I think you ought to have different bells—

Yardsley. I'll have a trolley-car gong for you, if it 'll only make you do the work properly.   Have you got a bicycle bell?

Mrs. Perkins. Yes ; that will do nicely for the curtain, and the desk push-button bell will do for the front-door bell.   Have you got that in your mind, Teddy dear?

Perkins. I feel as if I had the whole bicycle in my mind.   I can feel the wheels.   Bike for curtain, push for front door.   That's all right. I wouldn't mind pushing for the front door myself.   All ready?   All right.   In the absence of the bicycle bell, I'll be its under-study for once.   B-r-r-r-r-r-r !   [*Raises curtain.*

Yardsley. Now, Mrs. Perkins, begin with "I wonder why—"

Mrs. Perkins (*rehearsing*). I wonder why it is that once a woman gives her heart into another's keeping— (*Bell.*) Ah, the bell.   It must be he at last.   He is late this evening.

Enter Miss Andrews *as maid, with card on tray.*

Miss Andrews. Lady Amaranth, me luddy.

Yardsley. Lydy, Miss Andrews, lydy—not luddy.

Miss Andrews. Lydy Amaranth, me lady.

Yardsley. And please be consistent with your dialect. If it's Lydy Amaranth, it's Lydy Ellen.

Miss Andrews. Lydy Amaranth, me lydy.

Mrs. Perkins. What? Lydy Amaranth? She?

Yardsley. Oh dear! Excuse me, Mrs. Perkins, but you are not the maid, and cockney isn't required of you. You must not say lydy. Lady is—

Mrs. Perkins (resignedly). What? Lady Amaranth? She? What can she want? Show her up.   [*Exit* Miss Andrews.

Perkins. That's a first-class expression for an adventuress. *Show her up!* Gad! She ought to be shown up.

Mrs. Perkins. What can she want?

Enter Mrs. Bradley.

Mrs. Bradley. Ah, my dear Lady Ellen! What delight to find you at home! (*Aside.*) He is not here, and yet I could have sworn—

Mrs. Perkins. To what am I to attribute

this pleasure, Lady Amaranth? I do not presume to think that you have come here without some other motive than that of a mere desire to see me. I do not suppose that even you pretend that since the contretemps of Tuesday night at the Duchess of Barncastle's our former feeling—

Mrs. Bradley. Ellen, I have come to tell you something. To save you from a vile conspiracy.

Mrs. Perkins. I am quite well able, Lady Amaranth, to manage my own affairs—

Mrs. Bradley. But you do not know. You love Lord Muddleton—

Mrs. Perkins (toying with her fan). Oh! Indeed! And who, pray, has taken you into my confidence? I was not aware—

Mrs. Bradley. Hear me, Ellen—

Mrs. Perkins. Excuse me, Lady Amaranth! but you have forgotten that it is only to my friends that I am known as—

Mrs. Bradley. Then Lady Ellen, if it must be so. I know what you do not—that Henry Cobb is an escaped convent—

Yardsley. Convict, not convent.

Mrs. Bradley. Is an escaped convict, and—

Mrs. Perkins. I am not interested in Henry Cobb.

Mrs. Bradley. But he is in you, Ellen Abercrombie. He is in you, and with the aid of Fenderson Featherhead—

> [*Bell.* Perkins *lets curtain drop half-way,*
> *but remembers in time, and pulls it up*
> *again.*

Perkins. Beg pardon.   String slipped.

Mrs. Bradley. Too late.   Oh, if he had only waited!

Enter Miss Andrews.

Miss Andrews. Mr. Featherhead, Leddy Eilen.

Yardsley. Ellen, Ellen ; and lydy, not leddy.

Mrs. Bradley. Hear me first, I beg.

Mrs. Perkins. Show him in, Mary.   Lady Amaranth, as you see, I am engaged.   I really must be excused.   Good-night.

Mrs. Bradley (aside). Foiled! Muddleton will be exposed.   Ah, if I could only have broken the force of the blow!   (*Aloud.*) Lady Ellen, I will speak.   Fenderson Featherhead—

Enter Bradley *and* Barlow *together.*

Both. Is here, Lady Amaranth.

[*Each tries to motion the other off the stage.*

Yardsley. What the deuce does this mean? What do you think this play is—an *Uncle Tom* combination with two Topsys?

Barlow. I told him to keep out, but he said that Fenderson Featherhead was his cue.

Bradley (*indignantly*). Well, so it is; there's the book.

Yardsley. Oh, nonsense, Brad! Don't be idiotic. The book doesn't say anything of the sort.

Bradley. But I say it does. If you—

Barlow. It's all rot for you to behave like this, Bradley.

Perkins. Isn't it time something happened to the curtain? The audience will get panicky if they witness any such lack of harmony as this. I will draw a veil over the painful scene. B-r-r-r-r. (*Drops curtain.*) B-r-r-r-r.

[*Raises it again.*

Yardsley. We won't dispute the matter, Bradley. You are wrong, and that's all there is about it. Now do get off the stage and let us go ahead.   Perkins, for Heaven's sake, give that curtain a rest, will you?

Perkins. I was only having a dress-rehearsal on my own account, Bob.   Bike bell, curtain. Push bell, front door.   Trolley gong, nothing—

Bradley. Well, if you fellows won't—

Yardsley (*taking him by the arm and walking him to side of stage*). Never mind, Brad; you've made a mistake, that's all.   We all make mistakes at times.   Get off, like a good fellow.   You don't come on for ten minutes yet. (*Exit* Bradley, *scratching his head in puzzled meditation.*)   Go ahead now, Barlow.

Mrs. Bradley. But, Mr. Yardsley, Edward has—

Yardsley. We'll begin with your cue, Mrs. Bradley.   Fenderson Featherhead—

Barlow. Is here, Lady Amaranth.

Mrs. Bradley. But—"

Yardsley. No, no!   Your word isn't "but," Mrs. Bradley.   It's (*consulting book*)—it's : " Insolent!   You will cross my path once too often, and then—

Enter Bradley.

Mrs. Bradley. I know that, but I don't say that to him!

Bradley. Of course not. She says it to me.

Barlow. Well, of all the stupidity—

Perkins. Another unseemly fracas. Another veil. B-r-r-r-r. (*Drops curtain.*) There may be a hitch in the play, but there won't be in this curtain. I tell you that right now. B-r-r-r-r.

[*Raises curtain.*

Mrs. Perkins. Well, I don't pretend to understand the difficulty. She certainly does say that to Featherhead.

Barlow. Of course!—it's right there in the book.

Bradley. That's exactly what I say. It's in the book ; but you would come on.

Barlow. Well, why shouldn't I ?

Enter Miss Andrews.

Miss Andrews. What seems to be the trouble?

Perkins. I give it up. Collision somewhere up the road.

Yardsley (*turning over the leaves of the*

play-book). Oh, I see the trouble—it's all right. Bradley is mixed up a little, that's all. " Fenderson Featherhead " is his cue—but it comes later, Brad.

Bradley. Later? Well (*glances in book*)—no —it comes now.

Barlow. Are you blind? Can you read? See there!   [*Points into book.*

Yardsley. No—you keep still, Jack. I'll fix it. See here, Bradley. This is the place you are thinking of. When Cobb says to Lady Ellen " Fenderson Featherhead," you enter the room, and in a nervous aside you mutter: " What, he! Does he again dare to cross my path?" That's the way of it.

Barlow. Certainly — that's it, Brad. Now get off, and let me go on, will you?

Mrs. Perkins. I'm sure it's a perfectly natural error, Mr. Bradley.

Mrs. Bradley. But he's right, my dear Bess. The others are wrong. Edward doesn't—

Bradley. I don't care anything about it, but I'm sure I don't know what else to do. If I am to play Fenderson—

Barlow (*in amazement*). You?

Yardsley (*aghast*). Fenderson? By all that is lovely, what part have you learned?

Bradley. The one you told me to learn in your message—Featherhead, of course.

Barlow. But that's my part!

Mrs. Perkins. Of course it is, Mr. Bradley. Mr. Barlow is to be—

Mrs. Bradley. But that's what Edward was told. I saw the message myself.

Yardsley (*sinking into a chair dejectedly*). Why, Ed Bradley! I never mentioned Featherhead. You were to be Muddleton!

Bradley. Me?

Mrs. Bradley. What?

Yardsley. Certainly. There's nothing the matter with Barlow, and he's cast for Featherhead. You've learned the wrong part!

Bradley (*searching his pockets*). Here's the telegram. There (*takes message from pocket*), read that. There are my instructions.

Yardsley (*grasps telegram and reads it. Drops it to floor*). Well, I'll be jiggered!

[*Buries his face in his hands.*

Mrs. Perkins (*picking up message and reading aloud*). "Can you take Fenderson's part

in to-night's show? Answer at once. Yardsley."

Barlow. Well, that's a nice mess. You
must have paresis, Bob.

Perkins. I was afraid he'd get it sooner or
later. You need exercise, Yardsley. Go pull
that curtain up and down a half-dozen times
and it 'll do you good.

Bradley. That telegram lets me out.

Mrs. Bradley. I should say so.

Perkins. Lets us all out, seems to me.

Yardsley. But — I wrote Henderson, not
Fenderson. That jackass of a telegraph oper-
ator is responsible for it all. "Will you take
Henderson's part?" is what I wrote, and
he's gone and got it Fenderson. Confound
his—

Mrs. Perkins. But what are we going to
do? It's quarter-past six now, and the curtain is to rise at 8.30.

Perkins. I'll give 'em my unequalled imitation of Sandow lifting the curtain with one
hand. Thus. [*Raises curtain with right hand*.

Yardsley. For goodness' sake, man, be serious. There are seventy-five people coming

here to see this performance, and they've paid for their tickets.

Mrs. Perkins. It's perfectly awful. We can't do it at all unless Mr. Bradley will go right up stairs now and learn—

Mrs. Bradley. Oh, that's impossible. He's learned nearly three hundred lines to-day already. Mr. Barlow might—

Barlow. I couldn't think of it, Mrs. Bradley. I've got as much as I can do remembering what lines I have learned.

Perkins. It would take you a week to forget your old part completely enough to do the other well. You'd be playing both parts, the way Irving does when he's irritated, before you knew it.

Yardsley. I'm sure I don't know what to do.

Perkins. Give it up, eh? What are you stage-manager for? If I didn't own the house, I'd suggest setting it on fire; but I do, and it isn't fully insured.

Mrs. Perkins. Perhaps Miss Andrews and Mr. Yardsley could do their little scene from *Romeo and Juliet.*

Mrs. Bradley. Just the thing.

Yardsley. But I haven't a suitable costume.

Perkins. I'll lend you my golf trousers, and Bess has an old shirt-waist you could wear with 'em. Piece it out a little so that you could get into it, and hang the baby's toy sword at your side, and carry his fireman's hat under your arm, and you'd make a dandy-looking Romeo. Some people might think you were a new woman, but if somebody were to announce to the audience that you were not that, but the Hon. R. Montague, Esq., it would be all right and exceedingly amusing. I'll do the announcing with the greatest of pleasure. Really think I'd enjoy it.

Miss Andrews. I think it would be much better to get up Mrs. Jarley's waxworks.

Perkins. Oh dear, Miss Andrews, never. Mrs. Jarley awakens too many bitter memories in me. I was Mrs. Jarley once, and—

Yardsley. It must have been awful. If there is anything in life that could be more horrible than you, with your peculiar style of humor, trying to do Jarley, I—

Perkins. Oh, well, what's the odds what we

do ? We're only amateurs, anyhow. Yardsley can put on a pair of tight boots, and give us an impression of Irving, or perhaps an imitation of the Roman army at the battle of Philippi, and the audience wouldn't care, as long as they had a good supper afterwards. It all rests with Martenelli whether it's a go to-night. If he doesn't spoil the supper, it 'll be all right. I have observed that the principal factors of success at amateur dramatics are an expert manipulation of the curtain, and a first-class feed to put the audience in a good-humor afterwards. Even if Martenelli does go back on us, you'll have me with the curtain—

Mrs. Perkins. Thaddeus !

Yardsley. By Jove ! that's a good idea—we have got you. You can read Henderson's part !

Perkins. What—I ?

Barlow. Certainly.

Bradley. Just the very thing.

Miss Andrews. Splendid idea.

Perkins. Oh—but I say—I can't, you know. Nonsense ! I can't read.

Bardsley. I've often suspected that you

couldn't, my dear Thaddeus; but this time you must.

Perkins. But the curtain—the babies—the audience—the ushing—the fire department—it is too much.   I'm not an octopus.

Barlow (taking him by the arm and pushing him into chair).   You can't get out of it, Ted. Here—read up.   There—take my book.

> [*Thrusts play-book into his hand.*

Bradley. Here's mine, too, Thaddeus.   Read 'em both at once, and then you'll have gone over it twice.

> [*Throws his book into* Perkins's *lap.*

Perkins. I tell you—

Mrs. Perkins. Just this once, Teddy—please —for me.

Yardsley. You owe it to your position, Perkins.   You are the only man here that knows anything about anything.   You've frequently said so.   You were doing it all, anyhow, you know—and you're host—the audience are your guests—and you're so clever and—

Perkins. But—

> *Enter* Jennie.

Jennie. Dinner is served, ma'am.   [*Exit.*

Yardsley. Good! Perk, I'll be your under-
study at dinner, while you are studying up.
Ladies and gentlemen, kindly imagine that I
am host, that Perkins does not exist.   Come
along, Mrs. Bradley.   Miss Andrews, will you
take my other arm?   I'll escort Lady Amaranth and the maid out.   We'll leave the two
Featherheads to fight it out for the Lady Ellen.   By-by, Thaddeus; don't shirk.   I'll come
in after the salade course and hear you, and if
you don't know your lesson I'll send you to
bed without your supper

[*All go out, leaving* Perkins *alone.*
Perkins (*forcing a laugh*).   Ha! ha! ha!
Good joke, confound your eyes!   Humph!
very well.   I'll do it.   Whole thing, eh?   Curtain, babies, audience, host.   All right, my no-
ble Thespians, wait!   (*Shakes fist at the door.*)
I *will* do the whole thing.   Wait till they ring
you up, O curtain!   Up you will go, but then
—then will I come forth and read that book
from start to finish, and if any one of 'em
ventures to interfere I'll drop thee on their
most treasured lines.   They little dream how
much they are in the power of you and me!

Enter Jennie.

Jennie. Mrs. Perkins says aren't you coming to dinner, sir; and Mr. Yardsley says the soup is getting cold, sir.

Perkins. In a minute, Jennie. Tell Mrs. Perkins that I am just learning the last ten lines of the third act; and as for Mr. Yardsley, kindly insinuate to him that he'll find the soup quite hot enough at 8.30.

> [*Exit* Jennie. Perkins *sits down, and, taking up two books of the play, one in each hand, begins to read.*

[CURTAIN]

A PROPOSAL UNDER DIFFICULTIES

CHARACTERS:

ROBERT YARDSLEY,⎫ *suitors for the hand of Miss Andrews.*
JACK BARLOW,　　⎭
DOROTHY ANDREWS, *a much-loved young woman.*
JENNIE, *a housemaid.*
HICKS, *a coachman, who does not appear.*

The scene is laid in a fashionable New York drawing-room. The time is late in October, and Wednesday afternoon. The curtain rising shows an empty room. A bell rings. After a pause the front door is heard opening and closing. Enter Yardsley *through portière at rear of room.*

Yardsley. Ah! So far so good; but I wish it were over. I've had the nerve to get as far as the house and into it, but how much further my courage will carry me I can't say. Confound it! Why is it, I wonder, that men get so rattled when they're head over heels in love, and want to ask the fair object of their affections to wed? I can't see. Now I'm brave enough among men. I'm not afraid of anything that walks, except Dorothy Andrews, and generally I'm not afraid of her. Stopping runaway teams and talking back to impudent policemen have been my delight. I've even been courageous enough to submit a poem in person to the editor of a comic weekly, and yet here this afternoon I'm all of a tremble. And for what reason? Just because I've co-come to ask Dorothy Andrews to change her name to Mrs. Bob Yardsley; as if that were such an unlikely thing for her to do. Gad! I'm almost inclined to despise myself. (*Surveys himself in the mirror at one end of the room. Then walking up to it and peering intently at his reflection, he continues.*) Bah! you coward! Afraid of a woman—a sweet little woman like Dorothy. You ought to be ashamed of yourself, Bob Yardsley. *She* won't hurt you. Brace up and propose like a man —like a real lover who'd go through fire for her sake, and all that. Ha! That's easy enough to talk about, but how shall I put it?

That's the question. Let me see. How *do* men
do it? I ought to buy a few good novels and
select the sort of proposal I like ; but not having a novel at hand, I must invent my own.
How will it be? Something like this, I fancy.
(*The portières are parted, and* Jennie, *the maid,
enters.* Yardsley *does not observe her entrance.*)
I'll get down on my knees. A man on his
knees is a pitiable object, and pity, they say,
is akin to love. Maybe she'll pity me, and
after that—well, perhaps pity's cousin will
arrive. (*The maid advances, but* Yardsley *is
so intent upon his proposal that he still fails to
observe her. She stands back of the sofa, while
he, gazing downward, kneels before it.*) I'll
say : " Divine creature! At last we are alone,
and I—ah—I can speak freely the words that
have been in my heart to say to you for so
long—oh, so long a time." (Jennie *appears
surprised.*) " I have never even hinted at how
I feel towards you. I have concealed my love,
fearing lest by too sudden a betrayal of my
feelings I should lose all." (*Aside.*) Now for
a little allusion to the poets. Poetry, they
say, is a great thing for proposals. "You

know, dearest, you must know, how the poet has phrased it—' Fain would I fall but that I fear to climb.'   But now—now I must speak.

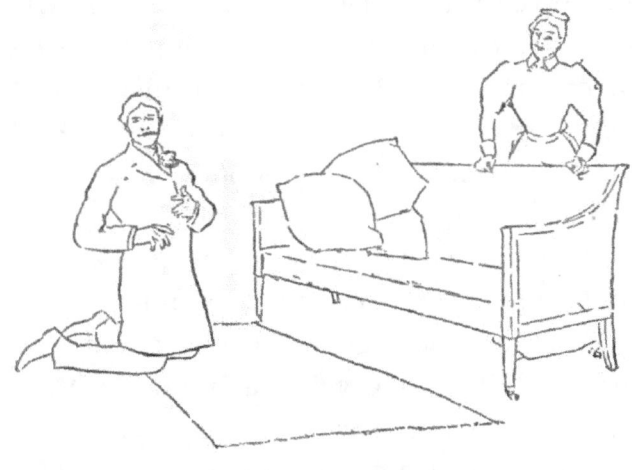

"' DIVINE CREATURE '"

An opportunity like this may not occur again. Will you—will you be my wife?"

[Jennie *gives a little scream of delight.*

Jennie. Oh, Mr. Yardsley, this is so suddenlike and unexpected, and me so far beneath you!

[Yardsley *looks up and is covered with confusion.*

Yardsley. Great Scott! What have I done?

Jennie. But of course it ain't for the likes of me to say no to—

Yardsley (rising). For Heaven's sake, Jennie—do be sensi— Don't—say— Jennie, why —ah— (*Aside.*) Oh, confound it! What the deuce shall I say? What's the matter with my tongue? Where's my vocabulary? A word! a word! my kingdom for a word! (*Aloud.*) Now, Jen—

Jennie (coyly). I has been engaged to Mr. Hicks, the coach gentleman, sir, but—

Yardsley. Good! good! I congratulate you, Jennie. Hicks is a very fine fellow. Drives like a — like a driver, Jennie, a born driver. I've seen him many a time sitting like a king on his box—yes, indeed. Noticed him often. Admired him. Gad, Jennie, I'll see him my-self and tell him ; and what is more, Jennie, I'll—I'll give Hicks a fine present.

Jennie. Yes, sir; I has no doubt as how you'll be doin' the square thing by Hicks, for, as I was a-sayin', I has been engaged like to him, an' he has some rights ; but I think as how, if I puts it to him right like, and tells him what a nice gentleman you are (*a ring is heard at the front door*), it'll be all right, sir. But there goes the bell, and I must run, Mr. Yardsley. (*Ecstatically kissing her hand.*) Bob!

Yardsley (*with a convulsive gasp*). Bob? Jennie! You—er—you misun— (Jennie, *with a smile of joy and an ecstatic glance at* Yardsley, *dances from the room to attend the door.* Yardsley *throws himself into a chair.*) Well, I'll be teetotally— Awh! It's too dead easy proposing to somebody you don't know you are proposing to. What a kettle of fish this is, to be sure! Oh, pshaw! that woman can't be serious. She must know I didn't mean it for her. But if she doesn't, good Lord! what becomes of me? (*Rises, and paces up and down the room nervously. After a moment he pauses before the glass.*) I ought to be considerably dishevelled by this. I feel as if I'd been drawn through a knot-hole—or—or dropped into a stone-crusher—that's it, a stone-crusher —a ten million horse-power stone-crusher. Let's see how you look, you poor idiot.

[*As he is stroking his hair and rearranging his tie he talks in pantomime at him-*

self in the glass. In a moment Jennie
ushers Mr. Jack Barlow *into the room.*

Jennie. Miss Andrews will be down in a
minute, sir.

[Barlow *takes arm-chair and sits gazing
ahead of him. Neither he nor* Yardsley
perceives the other. Jennie *tiptoes to
one side, and, tossing a kiss at* Yardsley,
retires.

Barlow. Now for it. I shall leave this
house to-day the happiest or the most miser-
able man in creation, and I rather think the
odds are in my favor. Why shouldn't they
be ? Egad ! I can very well understand how
a woman could admire me. I admire myself,
rather. I confess candidly that I do not consider myself half bad, and Dorothy has always
seemed to feel that way herself. In fact, the
other night in the Perkinses conservatory
she seemed to be quite ready for a proposal.
I'd have done it then and there if it hadn't
been for that confounded Bob Yardsley—

Yardsley (turning sharply about). Eh ?
Somebody spoke my name. A man, too.
Great heavens ! I hope Jennie's friend Hicks

isn't here. I don't want to have a scene with Hicks. (*Discovering* Barlow.) Oh—ah—why—hullo, Barlow! You here?

Barlow (*impatiently, aside*). Hang it! Yardsley's here too! The man's always turning up when he's not wanted. (*Aloud.*) Ah! why, Bob, how are you? What're you doing here?

Yardsley. What do you suppose — tuning the piano? I'm here because I want to be. And you?

Barlow. For the same reason that you are.

Yardsley (*aside*). Gad! I hope not. (*Aloud.*) Indeed? The great mind act again? Run in the same channel, and all that? Glad to see you. (*Aside.*) May the saints forgive me that fib! But this fellow must be got rid of.

Barlow (*embarrassed*). So'm I. Always glad to see myself—I mean you—anywhere. Won't you sit down?

Yardsley. Thanks. Very kind of you, I'm sure. (*Aside.*) He seems very much at home. Won't I sit down?—as if he'd inherited the chairs! Humph! I'll show him.

Barlow. What say?

Yardsley. I—ah—oh, I was merely remarking that I thought it was rather pleasant out to-day.

Barlow. Yes, almost too fine to be shut up in-doors. Why aren't you driving, or—or playing golf, or—ah—or being out-doors somewhere? You need exercise, old man; you look a little pale. (*Aside.*) I must get him away from here somehow. Deuced awkward having another fellow about when you mean to propose to a woman.

Yardsley. Oh, I'm well enough!

Barlow (*solicitously*). You don't look it—by Jove you don't. (*Suddenly inspired.*) No, you don't, Bob. You overestimate your strength. It's very wrong to overestimate one's strength. People — ah — people have died of it. Why, I'll bet you a hat you can't start now and walk up to Central Park and back in an hour. Come. I'll time you. (*Rises and takes out watch.*) It is now four ten. I'll wager you can't get back here before five thirty. Eh? Let me get your hat.

[*Starts for door.*

Yardsley (with a laugh). Oh no ; I don't bet
—after four.   But I say, did you see Billie
Wilkins?

Barlow. (returning in despair). Nope.

Yardsley (aside).
Now for a bit of
strategy. (*Aloud.*)
He   was   looking
for you at the club.
(*Aside.*)   Splendid
lie ! (*Aloud.*) Had
seats   for the—ah
—the Metropoli-
tan to-night. Said
he was looking for
you.   Wants you
to   go   with   him.

" ' I'll time you ' "

(*Aside.*)   That ought to start him along.

Barlow. I'll go with him.

Yardsley (eagerly). Well, you'd better let
him know at once, then.   Better run around
there and catch him while there's time.   He
said if he didn't see you before half-past four
he'd get Tom Parker to go.   Fine show to-
night. Wouldn't lose the opportunity if I

were you. (*Looking at his watch.*) You'll just about have time to do it now if you start at once.

> [*Grasps* Barlow *by arm, and tries to force
> him out.* Barlow *holds back, and is about
> to remonstrate, when* Dorothy *enters.
> Both men rush to greet her ;* Yardsley
> *catches her left hand,* Barlow *her right.*

Dorothy (*slightly embarrassed*). Why, how do you do—this is an unexpected pleasure—

both of you ? Excuse my left hand, Mr. Yardsley ; I should have given you the other if — if you'd given me time.

Yardsley. Don't mention it, I pray. The unexpectedness is wholly mine, Miss Andrews—I mean— ah—the pleasure is—

" ' START AT ONCE ' "

Barlow. Wholly mine.

Dorothy (*withdrawing her hands from both
and sitting down*). I haven't seen either of you

since the Perkinses dance. Wasn't it a charming affair?

Yardsley. Delightful. I—ah—I didn't know
that the Perkinses—

Barlow (interrupting). It was a good deal
of a crush, though. As Mrs. Van Darling said
to me, "You always meet—"

Yardsley. It's a pity Perkins isn't more of a
society man, though, don't you think?

Dorothy. O, I don't know. I've always found
him very pleasant. He is so sincere.

Barlow. Isn't he, though? He looked bored
to death all through the dance.

Yardsley. I thought so too. I was watch-
ing him while you were talking to him, Barlow, and such a look of ennui I never saw on
a man's face.

Barlow. Humph!

Dorothy. Are you going to Mrs. Van Darling's dinner?

Barlow. Yes; I received my bid last night.
You?

Dorothy. Oh yes!

Yardsley (gloomily). I can't go very well.
I'm—ah—engaged for Tuesday.

Barlow. Well, I hope you've let Mrs. Van Darling know. She's a stickler for promptness in accepting or declining her invitations. If you haven't, I'll tell her for you. I'm to see her to-night.

Yardsley. Oh no! Never mind. I'll—I'll attend to it.

Barlow. Oh, of course. But it's just as well she should know in advance. You might forget it, you know. I'll tell her; it's no trouble to me.

Dorothy. Of course not, and she can get some one to take your place.

Yardsley (*desperately*). Oh, don't say anything about it. Fact is, she—ah—she hasn't invited me.

Barlow. Ah! (*Aside.*) I knew that all along. Oh, but I'm clever!

Dorothy (*hastily, to relieve* Yardsley's *embarrassment*). Have you seen Irving, Mr. Yardsley?

Yardsley. Yes.

Barlow (*suspiciously*). What in? I haven't seen you at any of the first nights.

Yardsley (*with a grin*). In the grill-room at the Players.

Barlow (aside). Bah!

Dorothy (laughing). You are so bright, Mr. Yardsley.

Barlow (forcing a laugh). Ha, ha, ha! Why, yes—very clever that. It ought to have a Gibson picture over it, that joke. It would help it. Those Gibson pictures are fine, I think. Carry any kind of joke, eh?

Yardsley. Yes, they frequently do.

Dorothy. I'm so glad you both like Gibson, for I just dote on him. I have one of his originals in my portfolio. I'll get it if you'd like to see it.

> [*She rises and goes to the corner of the room, where there stands a portfolio-case.*

Yardsley (aside). What a bore Barlow is! Hang him! I must get rid of him somehow.

> [Barlow *meanwhile is assisting* Dorothy.

Yardsley (looking around at the others). Jove! he's off in the corner with her. Can't allow that, for the fact is Barlow's just a bit dangerous—to me.

Dorothy (rummaging through portfolio). Why, it *was* here—

Barlow. Maybe it's in this other portfolio.

Yardsley (joining them). Yes, maybe it is. That's a good idea. If it isn't in one portfolio maybe it's in another. Clever thought! I may be bright, Miss Andrews, but you must have observed that Barlow is thoughtful.

Dorothy (with a glance at Barlow). Yes, Mr. Yardsley, I have noticed the latter.

Barlow. Tee-hee! that's one on you, Bob.

Yardsley (obtuse). Ha, ha! Yes. Why, of course! Ha, ha, ha! For repartee I have always said—polite repartee, of course—Miss Andrews is— *(Aside.)* Now what the dickens did she mean by that?

Dorothy. I can't find it here. Let—me think. Where—can—it—be?

Barlow (striking thoughtful attitude). Yes, where can it be? Let me do your thinking for you, Miss Dorothy. *(Then softly to her.)* Always!

Yardsley (mocking Barlow). Yes! Let *me* think! *(Points his finger at his forehead and assumes tragic attitude. Then stalks to the front of stage in manner of burlesque* Hamlet.) Come, thought, come. Shed the glory of thy greatness full on me, and thus confound mine enemies.   Where the deuce is that Gibson?

Dorothy. Oh, I remember.   It's up-stairs.   I took it up with me last night.   I'll ring for Jennie, and have her get it.

Yardsley (*aside, and in consternation*). Jennie! Oh, thunder!   I'd forgotten her.   I do hope she remembers not to forget herself.

Barlow.   What say?

Yardsley. Nothing; only—ah—only that I thought it was very—very pleasant out.

Barlow.   That's what you said before.

Yardsley (*indignantly*). Well, what of it? It's the truth.   If you don't believe it, go outside and see for yourself.

> [Jennie *appears at the door in response to* Dorothy's *ring.   She glances demurely at* Yardsley, *who tries to ignore her presence.*

Dorothy. Jennie, go up to my room and look on the table in the corner, and bring me down the portfolio you will find there.   The large brown one that belongs in the stand over there.

Jennie (*dazed*). Yessum.   And shall I be bringin' lemons with it?

Dorothy. Lemons, Jennie?

Jennie. You always does have lemons with your tea, mum.

Dorothy. I didn't mention tea. I want you to get my portfolio from up-stairs. It is on the table in the corner of my room.

　　　　　　　[*Looks at* Jennie *in surprise.*

Jennie. Oh, excuse me, mum. I didn't hear straight.

　　　[*She casts a languishing glance at* Yardsley *and disappears.*

Yardsley (*noting the glance, presumably aside*). Confound that Jennie!

Barlow (*overhearing* Yardsley). What's that? Confound that Jennie? Why say confound that Jennie? Why do you wish Jennie to be confounded?

Yardsley (*nervously*). I didn't say that. I—ah—I merely said that—that Jennie appeared to be—ah—confounded.

Dorothy. She certainly is confused. I cannot understand it at all. Ordinarily I have rather envied Jennie her composure.

Yardsley. Oh, I suppose—it's—it's—it's natural for a young girl—a servant—sometimes to lose her—equipoise, as it were, on occasions.   If we lose ours at times, why not Jennie?   Eh?   Huh?

Barlow.   Certainly.

Yardsley.   Of course—ha—trained servants are hard to get these days, anyhow.   Educated people — ah — go into other professions, such as law, and—ah—the ministry—and—

Dorothy.   Well, never mind.   Let's talk of something more interesting than Jennie.   Going to the Chrysanthemum Show, Mr. Barlow?

Barlow.   I am;   wouldn't miss it for the world.   Do you know, really now, the chrysanthemum, in my opinion, is the most human-looking flower we have.   The rose is too beautiful, too perfect, for me.   The chrysanthemum, on the other hand—

Yardsley (*interrupting*).   Looks so like a football-player's head it appeals to your sympathies?   Well, perhaps you are right.   I never thought of it in that light before, but—

Dorothy (*smiling*).   Nor I;   but now that you mention it, it does look that way, doesn't it?

Barlow (*not wishing to disagree with* Dorothy).   Very much.   Droll idea, though.   Just like Bob, eh? Very, very droll. Bob's always dro—

Yardsley (interrupting). When I see a man walking down the Avenue with a chrysanthemum in his button-hole, I always think of a wild Indian wearing a scalp for decorative purposes.

> [Barlow *and* Dorothy *laugh at this, and during their mirth* Jennie *enters with the portfolio. She hands it to* Dorothy. Dorothy *rests it on the arm of her chair, and* Barlow *looking over one shoulder, she goes through it.* Jennie *in passing out throws another kiss to* Yardsley.

Yardsley (under his breath, stamping his foot). Awgh!

Barlow. What say?

> [Dorothy *looks up, surprised.*

Yardsley. I—I didn't say anything. My—ah—my shoe had a piece of—ah—

Barlow. Oh, say lint, and be done with it.

Yardsley (relieved, and thankful for the suggestion). Why, how did you know? It did, you know. Had a piece of lint on it, and I tried to get it off by stamping, that's all.

Dorothy. Ah, here it is.

Yardsley. What? The lint?

Barlow. Ho! Is the world nothing but lint to you? Of course not—the Gibson. Charming, isn't it, Miss Dorothy?

"'CHARMING, ISN'T IT?'"

Dorothy (*holding the picture up*). Fine. Just look at that girl. Isn't she pretty?

Barlow. Very.

Dorothy. And such style, too.

Yardsley (*looking over* Dorothy's *other shoulder*). Yes, very pretty, and lots of style. (*Softly.*) Very—like some one—some one I know.

Barlow (*overhearing*). I think so myself, Yardsley. It's exactly like Josie Wilkins. By-the-way—ah—how is that little affair coming along, Bob?

Dorothy (*interested*). What! You don't mean to say— Why, *Mister* Yardsley!

Yardsley (*with a venomous glance at* Barlow). Nonsense. Nothing in it. Mere invention of Barlow's. He's a regular Edison in his own way.

[Dorothy *looks inquiringly at* Barlow.

Barlow (*to* Yardsley). Oh, don't be so sly about it, old fellow! *Every*body knows.

Yardsley. But I tell you there's nothing in it. I—I have different ideas entirely, and you —you know it—or, if you don't, you will shortly.

Dorothy. Oh! Then it's some one else, Mr. Yardsley? Well, now I *am* interested. Let's have a little confidential talk together. Tell *us*, Mr. Yardsley, tell Mr. Barlow and me, and maybe—I can't say for certain, of course—but maybe we can help you.

Barlow (*gleefully rubbing his hands*). Yes, old man; certainly. Maybe we—*we* can help you.

Yardsley (*desperately*). You can help me, both of you—but—but I can't very well tell you how.

Barlow. I'm willing to do all I can for you, my dear Bob. If you will only tell us her name I'll even go so far as to call, in your behalf, and propose for you.

Yardsley. Oh, thanks.   You are very kind.

Dorothy. I think so too, Mr. Barlow. You are almost too kind, it seems to me.

Yardsley. Oh no; not too kind, Miss Andrews. Barlow simply realizes that one who has proposed marriage to young girls as frequently as he has knows how the thing is done, and he wishes to give me the benefit of his experience. (*Aside.*) That's a facer for Barlow.

Barlow. Ha, ha, ha!   Another joke, I suppose. You see, my dear Bob, that I am duly appreciative. I laugh. Ha, ha, ha! But I must say I laugh with some uncertainty. I don't know whether you intended that for a joke or for a staggerer. You should provide your conversation with a series of printed instructions for the listener. Get a lot of cards,

and have printed on one, "Please laugh";
on another, "Please stagger"; on another,
"Kindly appear confused." Then when you
mean to be jocose hand over the laughter
card, and so on. Shall I stagger?

Dorothy. I think that Mr. Yardsley meant
that for a joke. Didn't you, Mr. Yardsley?

Yardsley. Why, certainly. Of course. I
don't really believe Barlow ever had sand
enough to propose to any one. Did you, Jack?

Barlow (*indignant*). Well, I rather think I
have.

Dorothy. Ho, ho! Then you *are* an experi-
enced proposer, Mr. Barlow?

Barlow (*confused*). Why—er—well—um—I
didn't exactly mean that, you know. I meant
that—ah—if it ever came to the—er—the
test, I think I could—I'd have sand enough,
as Yardsley puts it, to do the thing properly,
and without making a—ah—a Yardsley of
myself.

Yardsley (*bristling up*). Now what do you
mean by that?

Dorothy. I think you are both of you horrid
this afternoon. You are so quarrelsome. Do

you two always quarrel, or is this merely a little afternoon's diversion got up for my especial benefit?

Barlow (with dignity). I never quarrel.

Yardsley. Nor I. I simply differ sometimes, that's all. I never had an unpleasant word with Jack in my life. Did I, Jack?

Barlow. Never. I always avoid a fracas, however great the provocation.

Dorothy (desperately). Then let us have a cup of tea together and be more sociable. I have always noticed that tea promotes sociability —haven't you, Mr. Yardsley?

Yardsley. Always. (*Aside.*) Among women.

Barlow. What say?

[Dorothy *rises and rings the bell for* Jennie.

Yardsley. I say that I am very fond of tea.

Barlow. So am I—here.

[*Rises and looks at pictures.* Yardsley *meanwhile sits in moody silence.*

Dorothy (returning). You seem to have something on your mind, Mr. Yardsley. I never knew you to be so solemn before.

Yardsley. I have something on my mind, Miss Dorothy. It's—

Barlow (*coming forward*). Wise man, cold weather like this. It would be terrible if you let your mind go out in cold weather without anything on it. Might catch cold in your idea.

Dorothy. I wonder why Jennie doesn't come? I shall have to ring again.

[*Pushes electric button again.*

Yardsley (*with an effort at brilliance*). The kitchen belle doesn't seem to work.

Dorothy. Ordinarily she does, but she seems to be upset by something this afternoon. I'm afraid she's in love. If you will excuse me a moment I will go and prepare the tea myself.

Barlow. Do; good! Then we shall not need the sugar.

Yardsley. You might omit the spoons too, after a remark like that, Miss Dorothy.

Dorothy. We'll omit Mr. Barlow's spoon. I'll bring some for you and me. [*She goes out.*

Yardsley (*with a laugh*). That's one on you, Barlow. But I say, old man (*taking out his watch and snapping the cover to three or four times*), it's getting very late—after five now. If you want to go with Billy Wilkins you'd

better take up your hat and walk.   I'll say
good-bye to Miss Andrews for you.

Barlow. Thanks.   Too late now.   You said
Billie wouldn't wait after four thirty.

Yardsley. Did I say four thirty?   I meant
five thirty.   Anyhow, Billie isn't over-prompt.
Better go.

Barlow. You seem mighty anxious to get
rid of me.

Yardsley. I?   Not at all, my dear boy—
not at all.   I'm very, very fond of you, but I
thought you'd prefer opera to me.   Don't you
see?   That's where my modesty comes in.
You're so fond of a good chat I thought you'd
want to go to-night.   Wilkins has a box.

Barlow. You said seats a little while ago.

Yardsley. Of course I did.   And why not?
There are seats in boxes.   Didn't you know
that?

Barlow. Look here, Yardsley, what's up, anyhow?   You've been deuced queer to-day.
What are you after?

Yardsley (*tragically*).   Shall I confide in you?
Can I, with a sense of confidence that you will
not betray me?

Barlow (*eagerly*). Yes, Bob. Go on. What is it? I'll never give you away, and I *may* be able to give you some good advice.

Yardsley. I am here to—to—to rob the house! Business has been bad, and one must live.   [Barlow *looks at him in disgust*.

" ' WHAT'S UP, ANYHOW?' "

Yardsley (*mockingly*). You have my secret, John Barlow. Remember that it was wrung from me in confidence. You must not betray me. Turn your back while I surreptitiously remove the piano and the gas-fixtures, won't you?

Barlow (*looking at him thoughtfully*). Yardsley, I have done you an injustice.

Yardsley. Indeed?

Barlow. Yes. Some one claimed, at the club, the other day, that you were the biggest donkey in existence, and I denied it. I was wrong, old man, I was wrong, and I apologize. You are.

Yardsley. You are too modest, Jack. You forget—yourself.

Barlow. Well, perhaps I do; but I've nothing to conceal, and you have. You've been behaving in a most incomprehensible fashion this afternoon, as if you owned the house.

Yardsley. Well, what of it? Do you own it?

Barlow. No, I don't, but—

Yardsley. But you hope to. Well, I have no such mercenary motive. I'm not after the house.

Barlow (*bristling up*). After the house? Mercenary motive? I demand an explanation of those words. What do you mean?

Yardsley. I mean this, Jack Barlow: I mean that I am here for—for my own reasons; but you—you have come here for the purpose of—

Dorothy *enters with a tray, upon which are the tea things.*

Barlow (about to retort to Yardsley, *perceiving* Dorothy). Ah! Let me assist you.

Dorothy. Thank you so much. I really believe I never needed help more. (*She delivers the tray to* Barlow, *who sets it on the table.* Dorothy, *exhausted, drops into a chair.*) Fan me—quick—or I shall faint. I've—I've had an awful time, and I really don't know what to do!

Barlow and *Yardsley (together).* Why, what's the matter?

Yardsley. I hope the house isn't on fire?

Barlow. Or that you haven't been robbed?

Dorothy. No, no; nothing like that. It's—it's about Jennie.

Yardsley (nervously). Jennie? Wha—wha—what's the matter with Jennie?

Dorothy. I only wish I knew. I—

Yardsley (aside). I'm glad you don't.

Barlow. What say?

Yardsley. I didn't say anything. Why should I say anything? I haven't anything to say. If people who had nothing to say would not insist upon talking, you'd be—

Dorothy. I heard the poor girl weeping down-stairs, and when I went to the dumb-waiter to ask her what was the matter, I heard —I heard a man's voice.

Yardsley. Man's voice?

Barlow. Man's voice is what Miss Andrews said.

Dorothy. Yes; it was Hicks, our coachman, and he was dreadfully angry about something.

Yardsley (sinking into chair). Good Lord! Hicks! Angry! At—something!

Dorothy. He was threatening to kill somebody.

Yardsley. This grows worse and worse! Threatening to kill somebody! D-did-did you o-over-overhear huh-huh-whom he was going to kuk-kill?

Barlow. What's the matter with you, Yardsley? Are you going to die of fright, or have you suddenly caught a chill?

Dorothy. Oh, I hope not! Don't die here, anyhow, Mr. Yardsley. If you must die, please go home and die. I couldn't stand another shock to-day. Why, really, I was nearly frightened to death. I don't know now but what

I ought to send for the police, Hicks was so violent.

Barlow. Perhaps she and Hicks have had a lovers' quarrel.

Yardsley. Very likely; very likely indeed. I think that is no doubt the explanation of the whole trouble. Lovers will quarrel. They were engaged, you know.

Dorothy (surprised). No, I didn't know it. Were they? Who told you?

Yardsley (discovering his mistake). Why— er—wasn't it you said so, Miss Dorothy? Or you, Barlow?

Barlow. I have not the honor of the young woman's confidence, and so could not have given you the information.

Dorothy. I didn't know it, so how could I have told you?

Yardsley (desperately). Then I must have dreamed it. I do have the queerest dreams sometimes, but there's nothing strange about this one, anyhow. Parlor-maids frequently do —er—become engaged to coachmen and butlers and that sort of thing. It isn't a rare occurrence at all. If I'd said she was engaged to Billie Wilkins, or to — to Barlow here—

Barlow. Or to yourself.

Yardsley. Sir? What do you mean to insinuate? That I am engaged to Jennie?

Barlow. I never said so.

Dorothy. Oh dear, let us have the tea. You quarrelsome men are just wearing me out. Mr. Barlow, do you want cream in yours?

Barlow. If you please; and one lump of sugar. (Dorothy *pours it out.*) Thanks.

Dorothy. Mr. Yardsley?

Yardsley. Just a little, Miss Andrews. No cream, and no sugar.

[Dorothy *prepares a cup for* Yardsley. *He is about to take it when—*

Dorothy. Well, I declare! *It's nothing but hot water! I forgot the tea entirely!*

Barlow (*with a laugh*). Oh, never mind. Hot water is good for dyspepsia.

[*With a significant look at* Yardsley.

Yardsley. It depends on how you get it, Mr. Barlow. I've known men who've got dyspepsia from living in hot water too much.

[*As* Yardsley *speaks the portière is violently clutched from without, and* Jennie's *head is thrust into the room. No one observes her.*

Barlow. Well, my cup is very satisfactory to me, Miss Dorothy.   Fact is, I've always been fond of cambric tea, and this is just right.

Yardsley (*patronizingly*). It *is* good for children.

Jennie (*trying to attract* Yardsley's *attention*). Pst !

Yardsley. My mamma lets me have it Sunday nights.

Dorothy. Ha, ha, ha !

Barlow. Another joke ?   Good.   Let me enjoy it too.   Hee, Hee !

Jennie. Pst !

[Barlow *looks around ;* Jennie *hastily withdraws her head.*

Barlow. I didn't know you had steam heat in this house.

Dorothy. We haven't.   What put such an idea as that into your head ?

Barlow. Why, I thought I heard the hissing

"' PST!'"

of steam, the click of a radiator, or something of that sort back by the door.

Yardsley. Maybe the house is haunted.

Dorothy. I fancy it was your imagination; or perhaps it was the wind blowing through the hall. The pantry window is open.

Barlow. I guess maybe that's it. How fine it must be in the country now!

[Jennie *pokes her head in through the portières again, and follows it with her arm and hand, in which is a feather duster, which she waves wildly in an endeavor to attract* Yardsley's *attention.*

Dorothy. Divine. I should so love to be out of town still. It seems to me people always make a great mistake returning to the city so early in the fall. The country is really at its best at this time of year.

[Yardsley *turns half around, and is about to speak, when he catches sight of the now almost hysterical* Jennie *and her feather duster.*

Barlow. Yes; I think so too. I was at Lenox last week, and the foliage was gorgeous.

Yardsley (*feeling that he must say something*).

Yes. I suppose all the feathers on the maple-trees are turning red by this time.

Dorothy. Feathers, Mr. Yardsley?

Barlow. Feathers?

Yardsley (with a furtive glance at Jennie). Ha, ha! What an absurd slip! Did I say feathers? I meant—I meant leaves, of course. All the leaves on the dusters are turning.

Barlow. I don't believe you know what you do mean. Who ever heard of leaves on dusters? What are dusters? Do you know, Miss Dorothy?

[*As he turns to* Miss Andrews, Yardsley *tries to wave* Jennie *away. She beckons with her arms more wildly than ever, and* Yardsley *silently speaks the words,* "Go away."

Dorothy. I'm sure I don't know of any tree by that name, but then I'm not a—not a what?

Yardsley (with a forced laugh). Treeologist.

Dorothy. What are dusters, Mr. Yardsley?

Barlow. Yes, old man, tell us. I'm anxious to find out myself.

Yardsley (aside). So am I. What the deuce are dusters, for this occasion only? (*Aloud.*)

What? Never heard of dusters? Ho! Why, dear me, where have you been all your lives? (*Aside.*) Must gain time to think up what dusters are. (*Aloud.*) Why, they're as old as the hills.

Barlow. That may be, but I can't say I think your description is at all definite.

Dorothy. Do they look like maples?

Yardsley (*with an angry wave of his arms towards* Jennie). Something — in fact, very much. They're exactly like them. You can hardly tell them from oaks.

Barlow. Oaks?

Yardsley. I said oaks. Oaks! O-A-K-S!

Barlow. But oaks aren't like maples.

Yardsley. Well, who said they were? We were talking about oaks—and—er—and dusters. We—er—we used to have a row of them in front of our old house at— (*Aside.*) Now where the deuce did we have the old house? Never had one, but we must for the sake of the present situation. (*Aloud.*) Up at—at— Bryn-Mawr—or at—Troy, or some such place, and — at — they kept the — the dust of the highway from getting into the house. (*With a sigh of relief.*)   And so, you see, they were called dusters.   Thought every one knew that.

[*As* Yardsley *finishes,* Jennie *loses her balance and falls headlong into the room.*

Dorothy (*starting up hastily*). Why, Jennie!

"'WHY, JENNIE!'"

Yardsley (*staggering into chair*). That settles it.   It's all up with me.

[Jennie *sobs, and, rising, rushes to* Yardsley's *side.*

Jennie. Save yourself; he's going to kill you!

Dorothy. Jennie! What is the meaning of this? Mr. Yardsley—can—can you shed any light on this mystery?

Yardsley (*pulling himself together with a great effort*). I? I assure you I can't, Miss Andrews.   How could I?   All I know is that somebody is—is going to kill me, though for what I haven't the slightest idea.

Jennie (*indignantly*). Eh? What! Why, Mr. Yardsley—Bob!

Barlow. Bob?

Dorothy. Jennie! Bob?

Yardsley. Don't you call me Bob.

Jennie. It's Hicks.   [*Bursts out crying.*

Barlow. Hicks?

Dorothy. Jennie, Hicks isn't Bob. His name is George.

Yardsley (in a despairing rage). Hicks be—

Dorothy. Mr. Yardsley!

Yardsley (pulling himself together again). Bobbed. Hicks be Bobbed. That's what I was going to say.

Dorothy. What on earth does this all mean? I must have an explanation, Jennie. What have you to say for yourself?

Jennie. Why, I—

Yardsley. I tell you it isn't true. She's made it up out of whole cloth.

Barlow. What isn't true? She hasn't said anything yet.

Yardsley (desperately). I refer to what she's going to say. I'm a—a—I'm a mind-reader, and I see it all as plain as day.

Dorothy. I can best judge of the truth of Jennie's words when she has spoken them,

Mr. Yardsley. Jennie, you may explain, if
you can. What do you mean by Hicks kill-
ing Mr. Yardsley, and why do you presume to
call Mr. Yardsley by his first name?

Yardsley (aside). Heigho! My goose is
cooked.

Barlow. I fancy you wish you had taken
that walk I suggested now.

Yardsley. You always were a good deal of
a fancier.

Jennie. I hardly knows how to begin, Miss
Dorothy. I — I'm so flabbergasted by all
that's happened this afternoon, mum, that I
can't get my thoughts straight, mum.

Dorothy. Never mind getting your thoughts
straight, Jennie. I do not want fiction. I
want the truth.

Jennie. Well, mum, when a fine gentleman
like Mr. Yardsley asks—

Yardsley. I tell you it isn't so.

Jennie. Indeed he did, mum.

Dorothy (impatiently). Did what?

Jennie. Axed me to marry him, mum.

Dorothy. Mr. Yardsley—asked—you—to—
to marry him?   [Barlow *whistles.*

Jennie (bursting into tears again). Yes, mum,
he did, mum, right here in this room. He got
down on his knees to me on that Proossian
rug before the sofa, mum. I was standin'
behind the sofa, havin' just come in to tell
him as how you'd be down shortly. He was
standin' before the lookin'-glass lookin' at
himself, an' when I come in he turns around
and goes down on his knees and says such an
importunity may not occur again, mum; I've
loved you very long; and then he recited
some pottery, mum, and said would I be his
wife.

Yardsley (desperately). Let me explain.

Dorothy. Wait, Mr. Yardsley; your turn will
come in a moment.

Barlow. Yes, it'll be here, my boy; don't
fret about that. Take all the time you need
to make it a good one. Gad, if this doesn't
strain your imagination, nothing will.

Dorothy. Go on, Jennie. Then what happened?

Yardsley (with an injured expression). Do
you expect me to stand here, Miss Andrews,
and hear this girl's horrible story?

Barlow. Then you know the story, do you, Yardsley? It's horrible, and you are innocent. My! you are a mind-reader with a vengeance.

Dorothy. Don't mind what these gentlemen say, Jennie, but go on.

[Yardsley *sinks into the arm-chair.* Barlow *chuckles;* Miss Andrews *glances indignantly at him.*

Dorothy. Pardon me, Mr. Barlow. If there is any humor in the situation, I fail to see it.

Barlow (*seeing his error*). Nor, indeed, do I. I was not—ah—laughing from mirth. That chuckle was hysterics, Miss Dorothy, I assure you. There are some laughs that can hardly be differentiated from sobs.

Jennie. I was all took in a heap, mum, to think of a fine gentleman like Mr. Yardsley proposing to me, mum, and I says the same. Says I, "Oh, Mr. Yardsley, this is so suddent like," whereat he looks up with a countenance so full o' pain that I hadn't the heart to refuse him; so, fergettin' Hicks for the moment, I says, kind of soft like, certingly, sir. It ain't for the likes o' me to say no to the likes o' him.

Yardsley. Then you said you were engaged to Hicks. You know you did, Jennie.

Barlow. Ah! Then you admit the proposal?

Yardsley. Oh Lord! Worse and worse! I—

Dorothy. Jennie has not finished her story.

Jennie. I did say as how I was engaged to Hicks, but I thought he would let me off; and Mr. Yardsley looked glad when I said that, and said he'd make it all right with Hicks.

Yardsley. What? I? Jennie O'Brien, or whatever your horrible name is, do you mean to say that I said I'd make it all right with Hicks?

Jennie. Not in them words, Mr. Yardsley; but you did say as how you'd see him yourself and give him a present. You did indeed, Mr. Yardsley, as you was a-standin' on that there Proossian rug.

Dorothy. Did you, Mr. Yardsley?

[Yardsley *buries his face in his hands and groans.*

Barlow. Not so ready with your explanations now, eh?

Dorothy. Mr. Barlow, really I must ask you

not to interfere. Did you say that, Mr. Yardsley?

Yardsley. I did, but—

Dorothy (*frigidly*). Go on, Jennie.

Jennie. Just then the front-door bell rings and Mr. Barlow comes, and there wasn't no more importunity for me to speak; but when I got down-stairs into the kitchen, mum, Mr. Hicks he comes in, an' (*sobs*)—an' I breaks with him.

Yardsley. You've broken with Hicks for me?

Jennie. Yes, I have—but I wouldn't never have done it if I'd known—boo-hoo—as how you'd behave this way an' deny ever havin' said a word. I—I—I l-lo-love Mr. Hicks, an' I—I hate you—and I wish I'd let him come up and kill you, as he said he would.

Dorothy. Jennie! Jennie! be calm! Where is Hicks now?

Yardsley. That's so. Where is Hicks? I want to see him.

Jennie. Never fear for that. You'll see him. He's layin' for you outside. An' that, Miss Dorothy, is why I was a-wavin' at him an' sayin "pst" to him. I wanted to warn him, mum, of his danger, mum, because Hicks is very vi'lent, and he told me in so many words as how he was a-goin' to *do—him—up*.

Barlow. You'd better inform Mr. Hicks, Jennie, that Mr. Yardsley is already done up.

Yardsley. Do me up, eh? Well, I like that. I'm not afraid of any coachman in creation as long as he's off the box. I'll go see him at once.

Dorothy. No—no—no. Don't, Mr. Yardsley; don't, I beg of you. I don't want to have any scene between you.

Yardsley (*heroically*). What if he succeeds? I don't care. As Barlow says, I'm done up as it is. I don't want to live after this. What's the use. Everything's lost.

Barlow (*dryly*). Jennie hasn't thrown you over yet.

Jennie (*sniffing airily*). Yes, she has, too. I wouldn't marry him now for all the world—an'—and I've lost—lost Hicks. (*Weeps.*) Him as was so brave, an' looks so fine in livery!

Yardsley. If you'd only give me a chance to say something—

Barlow. Appears to me you've said too much already.

Dorothy (*coldly*). I—I don't agree with Mr. Barlow. You—you haven't said enough, Mr. Yardsley. If you have any explanation to make, I'll listen.

Yardsley (*looks up gratefully. Suddenly his face brightens. Aside*). Gad! The very thing! I'll tell the exact truth, and if Dorothy has half the sense I think she has, I'll get in my proposal right under Barlow's very nose. (*Aloud.*) My—my explanation, Miss Andrews, is very simple. I—ah—I cannot deny having spoken every word that Jennie has charged to my account. I did get down on my knees on the rug. I did say "divine creature." I did not put it strong enough. I should have said "divinest of *all* creatures."

Dorothy (*in remonstrance*). Mr. Yardsley!

Barlow (*aside*). Magnificent bluff! But why? (*Rubs his forehead in a puzzled way.*) What the deuce is he driving at?

Yardsley. Kindly let me finish. I did say "I love you." I should have said "I adore you; I worship you." I did say "Will you be my wife?" and I was going to add, "for if you will not, then is light turned into darkness for me, and life, which your 'yes' will render radiantly beautiful, will become dull, colorless, and not worth the living." That is what I was going to say, Miss Andrews—Miss Dorothy—when—when Jennie interrupted me and spoke the word I most wish to hear—spoke the word "yes"; but it was not her yes that I wished. My words of love were not for her.

Barlow (*perceiving his drift*). Ho! Absurd! Nonsense! Most unreasonable! You were calling the sofa the divinest of all creatures, I suppose, or perhaps asking the—the piano to put on its shoes and—elope with you. Preposterous!

Dorothy (*softly*). Go on, Mr. Yardsley.

Yardsley. I—I spoke a little while ago about sand—courage—when it comes to one's asking the woman he loves the greatest of all questions. I was boastful. I pretended that I had that courage; but—well, I am not as brave as I seem. I had come, Miss Dorothy, to say to you the words that fell on Jennie's

ears, and—and I began to get nervous—stage-
fright, I suppose it was—and I was foolish
enough to rehearse what I had to say—to you,
and to you alone.

Barlow. Let me speak, Miss Andrews.   I—

Yardsley. You haven't anything to do with
the subject in hand, my dear Barlow, not a
thing.

Dorothy. Jennie—what—what have you to
say?

Jennie. Me?   Oh, mum, I hardly knows
what to say!   This is suddenter than the
other; but, Miss Dorothy, I'd believe him, I
would, because— I — I think he's tellin' the
truth, after all, for the reason that—oh dear—
for—

Dorothy. Don't be frightened, Jennie.   For
what reason?

Jennie. Well, mum, for the reason that when
I said "yes," mum, he didn't act like all the
other gentlemen I've said yes to, and—and
k—kuk—kiss me.

Yardsley. That's it! that's it!   Do you suppose that if I'd been after Jennie's yes, and
got it, I'd have let a door-bell and a sofa

stand between me and—the sealing of the proposal?

Barlow (*aside*). Oh, what nonsense this all is! I've got to get ahead of this fellow in some way. (*Aloud.*) Well, where do I come in? I came here, Miss Andrews, to tell you—

Yardsley (*interposing*). You come in where you came in before—just a little late—after the proposal, as it were.

Dorothy (*her face clearing and wreathing with smiles*). What a comedy of errors it has all been! I—I believe you, Mr. Yardsley.

Yardsley. Thank Heaven! And—ah—you aren't going to say anything more, D—Dorothy?

Dorothy. I'm afraid—

Yardsley. Are you going to make me go through that proposal all over again, now that I've got myself into so much trouble saying it the first time—Dorothy?

Dorothy. No, no. You needn't—you needn't speak of it again.

Barlow (*aside*). Good! That's *his congé.*

Yardsley. And—then if I—if I needn't say it again?   What then?   Can't I have—my answer now?   Oh, Miss Andrews—

Dorothy (*with downcast eyes, softly*). What did Jennie say?

Yardsley (*in ecstasy*). Do you mean it?

Barlow. I fancy—I fancy I'd better go now, Miss—er—Miss Andrews.   I—I—have an appointment with Mr. Wilkins, and—er—I observe that it is getting rather late.

Yardsley. Don't go yet, Jack.   I'm not so anxious to be rid of you now.

Barlow. I must go—really.

Yardsley. But I want you to make me one promise before you go.

Dorothy. He'll make it, I'm sure, if I ask him.   Mr. Yardsley and I want you — want you to be our best man.

Yardsley. That's it, precisely.   Eh, Jack?

Barlow. Well, yes. I'll be—second-best man. The events of the afternoon have shown my capacity for that.

Yardsley, Ah!

Barlow. And I'll show my sincerity by wearing Bob's hat and coat into the street

now and letting the fury of Hicks fall upon
me.

Jennie. If you please, Miss Dorothy—I—I
think I can attend to Mr. Hicks.

Dorothy. Very well. I think
that would be better. You
may go, Jennie.

         [Jennie *departs.*

Barlow. Well, good-day. I
—I've had a very pleasant
afternoon, Miss — Andrews.
Thanks for the—the cambric
tea.

Dorothy. Good - bye, and
don't forget.

HICKS.

Barlow. I'm afraid — I
won't. Good-bye, Bob. I congratulate you
from my heart. I was in hopes that I should
have the pleasure of having you for a best man
at *my* wedding, but—er—there's many a slip,
you know, and I wish you joy.

    [Yardsley *shakes him by the hand, and* Bar-
       low *goes out. As he disappears through
       the portières* Yardsley *follows, and, hold-
       ing the curtain aside, looks after him un-*

til the front door is heard closing.   Then he turns about.   Dorothy looks demurely around at him, and as he starts to go to her side the curtain falls.

THE END

THE ODD NUMBER SERIES.

16mo, Cloth, Ornamental.

DOÑA PERFECTA. By B. Pérez Galdós. Translated by Mary J. Serrano. $1 00.

PARISIAN POINTS OF VIEW. By Ludovic Halévy. Translated by Edith V. B. Matthews. $1 00.

DAME CARE. By Hermann Sudermann. Translated by Bertha Overbeck. $1 00.

TALES OF TWO COUNTRIES. By Alexander Kielland. Translated by William Archer. $1 00.

TEN TALES BY FRANÇOIS COPPÉE. Translated by Walter Learned. 50 Illustrations. $1 25.

MODERN GHOSTS. Selected and Translated. $1 00.

THE HOUSE BY THE MEDLAR-TREE. By Giovanni Verga. Translated from the Italian by Mary A. Craig. $1 00.

PASTELS IN PROSE. Translated by Stuart Merrill. 150 Illustrations. $1 25.

MARÍA: A South American Romance. By Jorge Isaacs. Translated by Rollo Ogden. $1 00.

THE ODD NUMBER. Thirteen Tales by Guy de Maupassant. The Translation by Jonathan Sturges. $1 00.

Published by HARPER & BROTHERS, New York.

For sale by all booksellers, or will be mailed by the publishers, postage prepaid, on receipt of the price.

By JAMES LANE ALLEN

AFTERMATH. Part Second of "A Kentucky Cardinal." Square 32mo, Cloth, Ornamental, $1 00.

How sweet and clean and healthy such a story as "Aftermath." . . . It is delightful reading.—*N. Y. Press.*

A KENTUCKY CARDINAL. Illustrated by ALBERT E. STERNER. Square 32mo, Cloth, Ornamental, $1 00.

Mr. James Lane Allen has never shown more delicacy and refinement of feeling or a more sympathetic appreciation of the beauties of nature.—*N. Y. Tribune.*

THE BLUE-GRASS REGION OF KENTUCKY, and Other Kentucky Articles. Illustrated. 8vo, Cloth, $2 50.

Mr. Allen has a poetic touch, a full vocabulary, a frequent felicity of phrase.—*Critic,* N. Y.
The attractions of the sketches are in their simplicity and realism. Nothing is oversaid or overdrawn.—*Chicago Inter-Ocean.*

FLUTE AND VIOLIN, and Other Kentucky Tales and Romances. Illustrated. Post 8vo, Cloth, Ornamental, $1 50; Silk Binding, $2 25.

Shows that there was an imaginative height and a poetic depth to be touched which no previous hand had reached in this class of historic fiction.—*N. Y. Evening Post.*

PUBLISHED BY HARPER & BROTHERS, NEW YORK.

☞ *The above works are for sale by all booksellers, or will be mailed by the publishers, postage prepaid, on receipt of the price.*

HARPER'S AMERICAN ESSAYISTS.

With Portraits. 16mo, Cloth, $1 00 each.

BY LAURENCE HUTTON

OTHER TIMES AND OTHER SEASONS. With Portrait. 16mo, Cloth, Ornamental, $1 00.

PORTRAITS IN PLASTER. From the Collection of LAURENCE HUTTON. 8vo, Cloth, Ornamental, Large Paper, Uncut Edges and Gilt Top, $6 00.

LITERARY LANDMARKS OF JERUSALEM. Illustrated. Post 8vo, Cloth, Ornamental, 75 cents.

LITERARY LANDMARKS OF LONDON. (*New Edition.*) Illustrated with over 70 Portraits. Post 8vo, Cloth, Ornamental, $1 75.

LITERARY LANDMAKS OF EDINBURGH. Illustrated. Post 8vo, Cloth, Ornamental, $1 00.

CURIOSITIES OF THE AMERICAN STAGE. With Copious and Characteristic Illustrations. Crown 8vo, Cloth, Ornamental, Uncut Edges and Gilt Top, $2 50.

FROM THE BOOKS OF LAURENCE HUTTON. With Portrait. 16mo, Cloth, Ornamental, $1 00.

EDWIN BOOTH. Illustrated. 32mo, Cloth, Ornamental, 50 cents.

PUBLISHED BY HARPER & BROTHERS, NEW YORK.

☞ *For sale by all booksellers, or will be mailed by the publishers, postage prepaid, on receipt of the price.*

Reprint Publishing

FOR PEOPLE WHO GO FOR ORIGINALS.

This book is a facsimile reprint of the original edition. The term refers to the facsimile with an original in size and design exactly matching simulation as photographic or scanned reproduction.

Facsimile editions offer us the chance to join in the library of historical, cultural and scientific history of mankind, and to rediscover.

The books of the facsimile edition may have marks, notations and other marginalia and pages with errors contained in the original volume. These traces of the past refers to the historical journey that has covered the book.

www.reprintpublishing.com